THE KISS GOODNIGHT

Novella
REVISED

CAROL GOODNIGHT

Copyright © 2015 CAROL GOODNIGHT

All rights reserved.

ISBN:099715280X
ISBN-13:9780997152807

This book is a work of fiction. Names, characters, places and incidents either are the product of the author's imagination or are used fictitiously. Any resemblance to actual persons, living or dead, or to actual events or locales is entirely coincidental.

THE FLAME

Demure the splendid orb of night
Embraced in redolent bliss
In shadow brood of past delight
Suspend on rim abyss

Empty echoes paw the sea
In search what once so fair
Yearning faded memory
Murmured ripples break the snare

Unquenched thirst of heart's desire
Sullen effort fought to tame
But embers fueled the famished fire
To hasten now the raging flame

CAROL GOODNIGHT

ACKNOWLEDGMENTS

KELLY WILLIAMSON
AIDAN RUTH
LILY BURHENNE
HOWARD FRIES (BIGH)
PATRICIA PAHULA
JAMES BRINDLEY

THE KISS GOODNIGHT

CHAPTER 1

Portofino, Italy

The full moon glistened on the harbor of Portofino with a cool, detached silence. Its long, deep shadows coiled dark tendrils in the pale glimmer as a soft breeze murmured unwelcome memories to the sleeping Carolyn Wingate.

She woke with a start, glanced around, and reached for the revolver hidden under her pillow. Pale beams lit the way as her silent footsteps followed a scratching noise to the edge of the deck.

Andrew would never find her in this small village, she thought, as she remembered the evil in his eyes when he'd choked her almost to death. She was safe now.

"Only a stick," she said as she looked over the railing to see a branch scraping against the hull.

She stared into the darkness following the pinpoints of light dotting the forested cliffs off in the distance as they reflected in long wavy beams stretching far out into the bay.

A cloud drifted over the moon darkening everything to a grey scale before moving on.

"Witchy Pitchfork," she said with a pained smile as the moon revealed herself once again.

The memory had softened over the last months. But just a bit. Since her brother Mike's death, Carolyn couldn't bare to look at the moon.

"That's a witch stirring a pot," she remembered them shouting as children as they gazed at the dark patches on its surface.

Carolyn sighed.

It was after midnight when she'd finished staining the teak on her new yacht, The Kiss Goodnight. She'd dozed off on the large cushioned lounge at the stern a few times already, but she hadn't had a good night's sleep since before her brother passed away.

Nestled back into the lounge cushions, Carolyn watched the tall houses in varying shades of red and gold lining the wharf glow a muted pastel in the darkness.

Distance had been all that mattered then, she remembered as her heartbeat slowed again.

After touring France for a few weeks with no sign of Andrew, Carolyn looked forward instead of over her shoulder. And when she'd read the ad for the yacht, and flown to Italy to see it, she realized she'd found a place she'd hadn't even known she'd been looking for.

The shadow of Castella Brown, a centuries old castle perched high on the promontory, watched over the peaceful bay satisfied her days as a military bastion were over. Her only invaders these days were tourists, sweaty and tired from the hike up to her gate. Relaxed in its looming darkness, Carolyn found comfort in the glimmer of the ankle chain her brother sent her before he'd passed away.

Open your heart ~ Look within, the locket read.

He'd always told her she had an inner strength.

Small boats tied up in lines of four or five deep on the opposite side of the bay glinted with color as they bobbed in the marina lights. Their gaily painted hulls coordinated and contrasted with the tall houses lining the harbor.

The larger modern yachts anchored to the left of the harbor - not so much in discrimination against the tiny workaday fishing boats, they would say if asked - but because the channel was deeper.

The truth was no doubt a little of both.

One 150-foot beauty hosted a loud party with chic people laughing and dancing to an on-board band, while another close to it rested silent, the people having gone off to shore.

Then there was The Kiss Goodnight, a classic old sailboat with style and grace.

Astounded when she'd first laid eyes on her, it seemed unnatural to be as love-smitten with an inanimate object as much as Carolyn was with this yacht. A psychologist would have chalked it up to loneliness and the inability to trust in love. Devastated by her brother's death, and the sheer terror from her experience with Andrew, the psychologist would have been on point.

But whatever the reason, Carolyn was in love.

This old gal outclasses them all! And she'd stop work to confirm her opinion every time a new boat entered the harbor.

The Kiss Goodnight was a forty-two-foot Gulet, a schooner-styled yacht made the old world way on the coast of Turkey near Bodrum. Her graceful style, sharp bow, broad beam, and rounded aft had been developed for the Mediterranean waters in Byzantium times.

A slick black lower hull, trimmed by a small white line of detail separated it from the rich dark mahogany that continued topside. When her classic white sails were at full sail, Carolyn noticed more than a few gaping-mouthed stares.

She'd transformed the stern into a large white cushioned lounge. A canvas canopy covered the area like a tent and provided much needed shade from the burning Mediterranean sun.

Carolyn nestled deeper in the cushions. The hard work she'd been doing to restore the yacht to its former beauty had consumed her for the last week. Now that she was safe, she kept busy and tried not to think about Andrew.

Peter crossed her mind often, and she'd wonder how he was doing. He'd been inconsolable after Andrew murdered her friend Sandy, his wife. Carolyn wracked her brain trying to figure out why he'd been so cruel yet go to such lengths to destroy her and kill her friend when she'd walked away

Their breakup had been Andrew's fault. He'd expected her to tolerate his abuse. And he couldn't get over the fact she'd left him.

When his rage turned murderous, he forced Carolyn to run and hide.

As the rhythmic waves lapped against the hull, she looked around the bay almost happy that he had.

A soft ping drifted from the cabin to break the stillness.

Carolyn headed to the fridge for cold water, annoyed that she'd received a junk email already. She'd just opened the account that afternoon.

Another ping sounded.

"Hm?" she said as she walked to the desk.

Another ping.

As she opened the first email, a paralyzing panic spread through her body.

I will find you bitch!

Carolyn's eyes bugged out as she whirled around staring into the darkness. Her jaw tightened on a muffled groan while fear twisted through her like a knife. The soft pings kept coming as she stumbled to the closest chair and set down her glass of water. Her eyes darted around the room and the hair on her scalp pulled upward. Unable to move, she sat frozen as her illusion of safety eroded further with every ping.

"No!" She reached over and jerked the cord from the plug. "No!"

She sunk back into the chair, subdued, with her limp arms dangling to the floor.

I will find you bitch! I will find you! The words ran through her mind.

Wait... I will find you. He doesn't know where I am!

Carolyn took a deep breath and sighed. Her hands trembled as she reached for the glass of water. She choked down a gulp and then headed back to the lounge.

She pulled a pillow behind her and sat staring out into the night. The muscles in her neck tightened as if invisible hands were still trying to strangle her. Every horrible incident replayed in her mind until they became unorganized in blackness. Near dawn her breathing became erratic and then calm before she drifted off to the shadowy realm of her dreams.

CHAPTER 2

The next afternoon Carolyn sat in the sun with Augie on the patio overlooking his vineyard. She'd arranged to meet him to pick up a float valve he'd purchased but forgot to install on the yacht before he'd sold it to her. After only a month and some odd days, she knew him well enough to know he would distract her with a story. Tired from little sleep, and in need of a diversion to stop the fearful thoughts of Andrew's words, she sat back to listen.

Augie arched one of his dark bushy eyebrows that contrasted with his head full of thick white hair and began the story of how the elegant vessel she'd purchased came into his life.

"I took the wife on the anniversary trip of her dreams," he started.

Carolyn took a long sip of cold lemonade. Her face wrinkled.

"More sugar?" he asked.

"No, I'm fine," she answered.

"Being a devout Catholic, the wife wanted to visit the seven ancient churches of the Bible in Turkey. So for our tenth anniversary, I surprised her with the trip.

Now, I'm not particularly interested in churches, mind you, but I needed to reward her hard work in helping bring the family vineyard back to a profitable operation.

That little gal worked alongside of me day and night and bore me two sons. The future of the vineyard looked bright in a large part due to her, and I thought it would be wonderful for our sons to inherit it someday, just as I had."

"I'm not a completely selfless man, you know. So, I managed a trip to Bodrum during our visit to the Turkish coast. And after a short half-day cruise, I fell in love with Eleganza.

It seemed to have that effect on people.

But, Eleganza?

She tilted her head to shield her eyes from the sun.

She was thinking it sounded like Gonzo on the Muppets as her mind wandered while Augie yammered on.

Carolyn knew from the first moment she saw her she'd buy the yacht. She'd name her The Kiss Goodnight, thinking back to her fondest memory of both her brother and her mother. The name would be a small attempt at keeping that memory alive in her heart forever.

Augie kept on with his story.

"I sent the wife home, bought her, and then sailed her home by myself."

'Prendendo il suo buon vecchio tempo maledetto, (Taking your good-old damn time) the wife would yell when the subject came up. She was crazy jealous of her from that first day until the day she died many years later."

"She said I'd get a gleam in my eye when I talked about her smooth mahogany hull. And about how I loved rubbing soft cloths of oil on her rich teak floors and smooth perfect walls whenever I could sneak away to her," he sighed.

He halted his story for a moment as he looked over the lush hillside full of grapevines as if remembering.

Then he chuckled. "That was, until the day she grew

sick to death of hearing about it and held up a knife. She yelled "Ti darò una Eleganza (I'll give you an Eleganza) while she was peeling potatoes. 'You ungrateful old sot,' she shouted. I'll run you through!'"

Augie raised his arms in the air and jumped back pretending he was avoiding a blade as he laughed.

"I knew she probably meant it too, so I kept my adoration of her private after. I adored that old gal."

Then he added with a laugh, "Both of them."

Augie went on to tell Carolyn how he loved working on his Elaganza.

"Your Eleganza, I mean," he'd added.

He loved the wonderful days of gliding like a god on the thin edge of blue heaven and the bluer sea. But this last year had been rough on him, he said. He'd realized he'd gotten too old and frail to sail alone, let alone keep up with the heavy maintenance on a wooden yacht.

After his second glass of wine, he'd speak bitterly about how his worthless sons had deserted him and gone off to Rome. Even though one son became a doctor, and the other was a decorated member of AISE, similar to the CIA in the United States.

"They think they're gonna come back here when I'm dead and gone and drink my wine and sail my boat. Over my dead body!" he said. "That's why I put Eleganza up for sale."

For the third time since she'd met him, he told her the story of how, before Carolyn answered his ad in the small local paper, the idea of selling to a female had never occurred to him.

"As is the old-world way," he said.

Third? Or is this the fourth time? Carolyn wondered.

"There was a softness in your voice that sounded caring and comforting, so I decided to meet with you, he'd always say.

His story went on... One look at her and Augie had made up his mind. Carolyn and his old girl were perfect for each other. He thought Carolyn's curves and fine lines were a fitting match to his favorite lady. He was too much of a gentleman to say those words to her, but he thought them nonetheless. So with mixed emotions he sold her, but with a promise from Carolyn that she would let him sail with her occasionally.

Augie tried to teach Carolyn everything he knew about sailing those first few short weeks. They cruised the coast from early morning until late in the evening every single day. Ombra, his faithful dog, always accompanied them. He'd stretch out on the back lounge, with his snout in the air as if he were an important Italian film star.

It was one of the finest times of his life, he'd told her more than once. His regret that neither of his sons had shown any interest in the things he loved, the vineyard or the yacht, was all the more painful by seeing how much Carolyn loved both. He'd found himself with a new regret.

"I should have had a daughter," he said to anyone who would listen.

After getting the OK from Augie to change the name from Eleganza to The Kiss Goodnight, Carolyn researched the procedure. She found that since time began, sailors have known the unluckiest ships are those that have defied Neptune, the god of the deep. Every vessel is recorded in the great ledger kept by Neptune himself and renaming a vessel is not to be taken lightly. If Neptune finds a vessel sailing his waters without being properly listed in his ledger, it will surely suffer his wrath, usually sooner rather than later.

The previous vessel name must be purged from the ledger and Neptune's memory. Every item bearing the vessel's name must be removed including erasing the name from the logs.

Carolyn made a thorough search, with Augie's help, and they packed up every item bearing the hideous name Eleganza. It was a little sad for Augie, but he loved the new name and agreed it was a much more fitting name for a yacht

THE KISS GOODNIGHT

belonging to Carolyn.

She put together a small party at the marina for the ceremony and invited her new friends and all of Augie's old friends. Augie contributed the very best sparkling wine from his vineyard as he wanted no problems for Carolyn from the deity beneath the sea.

With the small crowd looking on, she began the ceremony. She wrote the name, Eleganza, on a small metal ingot in water-soluble ink and went to the bow of Eleganza to begin the denaming ceremony.

"Oh mighty and great ruler of the seas and oceans, to whom all ships and we who venture upon your vast domain are required to pay homage, we implore you in your graciousness to expunge for all time from your records and recollection the name Eleganza, which has ceased to be an entity in your kingdom. As proof thereof, we submit this ingot bearing her name to be corrupted through your powers and forever be purged from the sea."

She dropped the ingot into the sea.

"In grateful acknowledgment of your munificence and dispensation, we offer these libations to your majesty and your court."

She poured half the bottle of sparkling wine into the sea, starting to the east and moving to the west. Saving the rest of that bottle to share with the small party on the dock, she opened a new bottle and continued with the rest of the ceremony.

When it was finished, Everyone on the dock raised a glass to her and Augie and shouted in a combination of English and Italian, "May your days be many and your troubles few. Fair winds and following seas."

Ramone, the dock boy, scampered on board with paint and a sling he'd devised for hanging off boats to paint touch-ups. But today he would decommission the Elaganza and proudly commission the new name.

Before they'd finished a second glass of sparkling wine, Ramone called out, "The Kiss Goodnight!" with a proud smile, pointing to his work with both arms while his legs dangled back and forth.

"Bellissimo!" Carolyn shouted. "Michaelango."

Everyone applauded while boarding The Kiss Goodnight. With a satisfied sigh, Carolyn looked over the harbor, her yacht, and her new friends.

I've done it. I'm safe. And as an extra bonus, I'm happy.

"Come on, everyone. Let's enjoy!"

Platters of cheese, grapes, savory and sweet pastries, and much more sparkling wine awaited them. Small tortas made with cheese, eggs, fresh herbs, and Swiss chard filled the large oblong mahogany dining table just in front of the lounge area. To one side of the table sat small flans filled with spinach, cheese, and mushrooms. In the middle of the table sat a big crock of Burrida, a fish stew made with fish, squid, tomatoes, and white wine.

Desserts filled the other side of the table. Zeppoli, deep-fried dough balls dusted with powdered sugar and filled with lemon pudding, Pistachio biscotti, Zuppa Inglese, an Italian version of trifle, and Cannoli, filled with sweet creamy ricotta cheese all awaited Carolyn and her guests.

"Oh, Carolyn, you must kiss me good night," said one of Augie's old friends, reaching out toward her. He'd found a shirt for the occasion, the first time she'd ever seen him wear one. Carolyn laughed and gave him a kiss on the forehead.

"No, no, girl, you come back here and I will show you how to kiss," he said, reaching for Carolyn.

She looked back. "You behave, or no more wine for you," she laughed.

Everyone feasted late into the night, eating, drinking, and laughing. The locals enjoyed the party, even though they thought the American was very odd for changing a perfectly good name. Especially *that* name.

Near dawn, with a heavy heart, Augie ceremoniously handed Carolyn the helm, kissed her on both cheeks, and then climbed back to the dock. She watched as he stood petting his ever-faithful Ombra, looking back for a long time to admire the yacht's silhouette by morning twilight. His eyes crinkled in a smile as his lip quivered and a tear dribbled down his day-old white beard. He gave a half-hearted wave. Ombra, glad to have his master's full attention once more, wagged his tail with some extra happy as they headed for home.

CHAPTER 3

Wind ripped through the streets of Portofino clattering the loose clay tile roofs of the old village. Sinister black clouds stirred in a frenzy, roiling and churning above Carolyn as she hurried toward the theatre. The sky grew more threatening with each step. The first crack of lightning slashed across the sky in a scorching jag of blue resembling the creeping veins of an old woman's hand.

Raw, slapping rain bit into her face as it unleashed itself in sheets of shredded gray. Carolyn shuddered and buried her neck in the collar of her sweater.

The torrent battered the cobbled pavement and splashed her ankles to the knee before rushing to gather in gullies and deluge down street. She pulled her sweater up over her head.

"Never! I never remember an umbrella," she chided herself.

A hunched-over bundle of raincoat with a makeshift newspaper hat ambled past, knocking into her before stopping to hold the door.

Drooping, moisture-laden branches dripped overhead to mix with the gray-brown run-off from a broken gutter before it drained over the soaking figure-the reward for his gallantry.

Their eyes met as she rushed past.

Even from that first moment, Carolyn was drawn this stranger. He met her glimpse into his sodden-newspaper covered eyes with a kindness, a warmth after a lifetime of winter.

THE KISS GOODNIGHT

Their mutual destination was a small theatre screening several Hitchcock films to celebrate one Hitchcock anniversary or another.

She wondered about the man, who'd also forgotten an umbrella, as he unwrapped his drenched coat.

He was handsome, on his own, and watching Hitchcock. Maybe he was a serial killer, she thought before laughing at herself. She doubted that serial killers watched movies in swanky Portofino theatres. Or did they?

After her experience with Andrew, Carolyn felt sure she could recognize a dangerous psychopath, even at a glance.

When she remembered his cold eyes and icy stare, she shuddered.

She didn't want to think about Andrew now. Or ever again. It'd been months since she'd left the states. Her old life was over and she was living a new life now.

After purchasing her ticket, Carolyn glanced toward the man again. He turned to catch her eye before she could look away. A genuine grin spread across his face. His warm blue eyes twinkled with amusement as if he knew a secret she didn't. A glimmer of wistfulness absorbed her as she felt him gazing at her.

He looked as if he may have been a writer or an artist. Or maybe just a dreamer.

As the thunder crashed once more, the handsome stranger spoke out in a genteel Charleston accent.

"I swaya, it's those damn Yankee cannons chasing me again," he said.

Carolyn giggled even though she was a Yankee and had always hated those references.

He shook his soaked raincoat to his side and cleared his throat.

"Allow me to introduce myself. Griffin P. Montgomery, at your service," he said, bowing from the waist.

"Please don't ask me about the P. I'd be loath to lie so early in our courtship."

Carolyn giggled again.

That was over a week ago, a lifetime it seemed. She'd met Griff for lunch every afternoon since. After the first few days she found herself with a tail-wagging friend as she waited at their regular sidewalk café. Carolyn found it charming that Griff carried treats in his pocket for the café owner's chubby beagle. The old dog sat next to her when Griff rounded the corner with his now-familiar jaunty gait and affable grin. He was the polar opposite of Andrew right down to his walk.

They'd sat in the café for hours, drinking coffee, talking of school, and work, and life. When Griff spoke of his many shenanigans he gleamed with the smile of a mischievous boy. But when he spoke of the hardships of life we all face, a kindness shone from his soul. He was like a diamond, rough and not yet cut, still with all the hard edges, but enough to glint his inner beauty.

As the long, lazy afternoons slipped into evenings, the beagle would head in for dinner whereupon the café owner would serve them wine instead of coffee.

The more Carolyn learned about Griff, the more she wanted to know. He was an artist and portrayed his world, at least in his stories, in an elaborate array of vivid color with either refined or garish structure. His tales dashed from the tranquility of a cricket's soothing cadence on the back porch of his Charleston cottage to the screeching crash of his car barreling through the front door of the local grocery store while on a search for fresh eggs and kale after an artistic all-nighter.

Carolyn's stories were pale by comparison. She left out the stories about her family and kept them about work. Her other stories regarding Andrew were distasteful and unnerving and didn't seem relevant in this setting. She was free of him and the almost forgotten misery that surrounded him.

Late one afternoon Griff invited Carolyn to view his latest painting.

"It's a work in progress, darlin'. It'll need many more layers before I'm happy with it."

He left an extra-large tip before he looked around and then plucked a rose from the climbing vine next to their table.

"For your hair," he said with a devilish grin.

They strolled side-by-side up the narrow cobbled streets until they came to a steep set of stairs. Griff stepped up and turned around.

"You'll need assistance for this climb, my dear," he said as he reached for Carolyn's hand.

"It's a rough go after a few glasses of the old vino," he laughed.

When he reached his hand to caress hers that first time, a spark of excitement compelled the blood in her veins to dance to the tip of her nerve endings where it resolved itself in a purring hum. She lifted her face to look at him. As he met her gaze, his glistening eyes shone the color of the Mediterranean during a storm. Dark flecks, like sea kelp crashing and churning, radiated an impishness that caused no alarm, but rather a warm comfort, like a dogged and frayed favorite sweater.

Carolyn stood paralyzed as their eyes locked. His head angled to the side as his lips came closer to hers. He leaned in until their foreheads touched. His over-long hair hung in tufts and tangles and blew wildly as he reached to caress her face.

The tips of his fingers tickled her earlobe as he slid them behind her head without a waiver of his stare. His hand rested on her neck as his thumb caressed her cheek.

She inhaled the craving moistness of his breath, surprised to find her own lips parted, and ran her fingers down his back to pull him closer until she could feel the beating of his heart against her chest.

She wanted to pull away, she didn't want...

She lost herself in the moment.

As his cheek touched hers, the ambient music of an old Italian love song drifting down the alley pulled her along in its wake. As his soft lips pressed against hers, the earth paused on its axis for a brief moment and the world around them disappeared altogether.

Griff's hand searched around the small of Carolyn's back as he pulled her body closer. As his fingers pressed into her, she felt embarrassed by her sudden desire. She hoped her flaming cheeks wouldn't give her away.

Griff groaned.

He pulled away from her lips and nuzzled a slow kiss along her neck. She felt weak in the knees, but didn't dare move. As he released his embrace, the world came back into focus and she gasped a quick breath. Griff stood smiling at her. Carolyn wrapped her hand in his and didn't say another word until they arrived at his apartment.

The first thing she noticed about his place was the mess. Different size canvas in various stages of progress lined one entire wall. A table that would rival any television crime scene contained squished tubes and palettes of gobbed color. Several shirts streaked with smears of cadmium red and Payne's gray laying on his bed would give a cleaning lady cause to call the cops and result in a subsequent search to find a body. It didn't look like there'd ever been a cleaning lady, however.

Off in the corner, in the buffered light of the matchstick blinds, stood an easel and a painting.

Carolyn's eyes widened as she stepped toward it.

"That's our table! That's us!" she said.

She reached out and waved her fingers above the paint. The couple at the table were holding hands. A fat beagle sat next to the man waiting for a treat.

"It is us, darlin'. I knew from get-go I'd be holding your hand one day," Griff said with a big grin.

For the next week or so, with their hands clenched, they sipped, chatted, and fed the beagle snacks. Carolyn limited kisses to quick hello and goodbye pecks. Until she was sure she was ready to get involved, she thought it best. The intensity of that first kiss had been overwhelming.

She wasn't sure when it happened. It might have started as far back as that day he stood in the rain and held the door. But whenever it occurred, falling for Griff had been as unnerving and exhilarating as getting on an old wooden rollercoaster.

Their cart had climbed slow... slow... agonizingly slow... but ever-so steady up those rickety tracks. Her heart raced forward as she leaned back in a vain attempt to keep things casual. She found herself stalled toward the top with an overwhelming anticipation.

If she could've turned back, would she have?

At some point she realized it was already too late.

She tried to convince herself that it would all be fine. They were friends. He was fun. Love was a silly notion.

Then she'd see Griff again, hold his hand, linger a kiss near his face, her stomach would lurch and the bottom would drop out as she flew and twisted around the hairpin turns.

She was smiling at the thought as Griff rounded the corner. His shadow crossed her face as he bent to kiss her forehead. He stood looking in her eyes before reaching up to smooth back her blowing hair.

"You know I'm falling in love with you, don't you darlin'?" he asked.

Carolyn smiled as her gaze drifted downward to hide her blush. He had to know she'd been feeling the same about him.

"It's true, darlin'. I've been giving it a lot of thought. You've been burrowing in my heart since the first day I rescued you from that storm. There was no warnin'. I fell in it like a badger hole in high grass and it's been like chiggers chewin' ever since.

Carolyn laughed.

Their crazy, heart-stopping roller-coaster ride was just about to take off. Anyone would have thought falling for a random stranger that turned out to be a psychopath would have taught her a lesson. But Carolyn closed her eyes and leaned in to kiss Griff's lips.

CHAPTER 4

Carolyn woke early to an easy breeze caressing her face. She opened her eyes to the awe and beauty of another Mediterranean sunrise as the quiet waves against the yacht nudged her toward a new day. She'd slept on the lounge in the stern with the cover furled back so she could fall asleep to the moon arcing across the sky while she wished on stars.

"Um," she said as she stretched out.

After the naming ceremony, she'd spent many days traveling along the coast looking for small coves to anchor and spend the night. She liked secluded places that shielded her from other people as well as the open sea. Many of the small bays and coves on the Ligurian coast of Italy fit her purposes nicely.

She motored the dinghy to the harbor and rented a small Vespa. Carolyn knew Italian traffic didn't have many rules and driving always unnerved her. She'd learned a few weeks earlier in Genoa to always take a moment to prepare mentally before taking to the road. Scooters buzzed between tiny cars, big cars, trucks, overloaded hay wagons with farmer's wives sitting precariously on top, horses with buggies, mules, bicycles, goats, and pedestrians sashaying around without a care in the world and absolutely no fear.

Driving requirements are guts and horns and everyone had plenty of both.

Honks, tire squeals, Italian phrases, and hand waving made traffic laws and signs unnecessary. Fortunately Portofino was not as crazy as the larger cities.

Carolyn headed up out of the small-town bustle on the narrow winding mountain road that corkscrewed back and forth through the thick forest.

Passing small wild patches of yellow kangaroo-paws with furry stems and tall gymea lilies with their flame flowers blooming, she smiled as she breathed in the fragrant air. As she rode higher, the air shed its humid salty notes and took on a deep earthiness emanating from the rich ochre soil.

She realized life was nothing more than a string of fragile and fleeting moments flitting through time like bows on the tail of a runaway kite. And she tried to soak in all the beauty she could.

The dim sound of a motor became louder and louder until she turned behind her to see a beat-up old car closing in on her. Carolyn pulled to the right side of the road to let the noisy piece of junk pass. The car behind her slowed and then stopped.

The driver stuck his head out of the half-open dirty window and smiled. But far from friendly, his smile was more of a crazy-eyed sneer. Carolyn took in a gasp as a chill gripped her heart.

Andrew sent him! She twisted the throttle and took off with her foot dragging in the gravel.

The crazy-eyed driver followed. When he caught up, he revved his engine as if he were going to run her down. Carolyn stomach dropped as she glanced over the cliff's edge while rounding the corner of a hairpin turn.

Loose stones kicked up from the scooter's wheels tumbled over the rocky edge. She made a quick right on the other side of the turn and pulled into the woods. While the driver slowed to make the turn, Carolyn shut off the engine and crouched in the tall weeds.

She could hear a maniacal laugh as the driver passed. He looked around and then sped up as if to catch up with her.

After considering turning back, she pulled the scooter from the weeds and headed toward Augie's place.

"I'll be damned!" she said as she pulled her purse straps around for an easier reach of the pistol.

As Carolyn drove the Vespa through the colonnade of tall cypress trees lining the long dusty driveway, she said a silent prayer of gratitude.

By the time Augie walked out to the little stone bench

between his front door and the entrance to the vineyard, she'd decided to keep the chase incident to herself.

She smiled when she saw Ombra sitting in his usual spot under Augie's arm to make for some easy head scratching.

She saw his head reaching up as he gave a quick double bark. His alert was helpful in greeting customers as few travelers ventured up this far, preferring to use the coast road unless they were planning to stop at the vineyard, Augie had told her.

The stone bench, Augie's informal greeting area, sat in front of an ancient wooden wagon full of huge, hand-blown demi-johns used to store wine. Basketry covered a few of the bottles while most of the woven reeds around the others were in various stages of disintegration from years of exposure to the hot Mediterranean sun. One long frayed rope wrapped around each bottleneck, tying them together in two rows, making them look like an old southern chain gang shackled together. One errant bottle had escaped. It lay in freedom on its side next to the bench.

The wagon itself, parked there "temporarily" years ago, had also seen better days. Wooden sections of the wheels had disintegrated in places, with only rusted metal rims holding them together. The charming vignette in front of Augie's huge saffron-colored stone-and-stucco house appeared staged *after* someone had emptied all the demijohns.

The house and the land had at one time been home to a secluded convent. Augie's ancestors had purchased it nine or ten generations back. Augie could never verify that handed-down story, however.

Attempts at plastering the old stone walls over the decades, to aid in keeping out wind, rain, and various pests, appeared to be a losing battle. With the stucco peeling off the front of the house, it left small gaps between the walls and the stone arch around the door. One of the front door's wrought iron gates was in a permanent state of welcome while the other gate was still on duty, keeping its half of the doorway secure.

When Carolyn reached the tall cypress trees, the turnoff to Augie's property, Ombre barked twice more. His sharp, deep bark echoed through the rolling hills of Augie's twenty-hectare vineyard and then on out over the ocean.

Carolyn saw Augie wave, knowing he'd be happy to see her.

Ombra had been a salve to the bitter loss of his wife, but it was no secret he'd been lonely for human companionship since she'd died. He'd often told Carolyn he considered himself as lucky in meeting her as he had been in finding Ombra.

She'd already heard the story twice of how his neighbor had invited him for Sunday dinner several weeks after his wife passed away, giving Augie his first glimpse of the pup. He was the runt of the litter, a Cane Corso, known for guarding, companionship, and hunting. Not too far descended from wolves, the mother had dug a small den under the back of the neighbor's barn. Her nice doghouse sat empty next to the house.

After Sunday dinner, Augie and his friend took a stroll to see the pups. Ombra, crowded out of the den by the larger pups, kept bumping his head on the bottom board of the barn wall. Augie wouldn't have even seen him, being coal black and hidden in the shadows, but for his pitiful yelp each time he hit his head.

Augie watched for a moment before bending down and swooping him up in one hand.

"I'll take this little shadow," he told the neighbor.

"I'll call him Ombra. What do you want for him?"

"He's yours, Augie. He's a runt. Probably wouldn't a made it anyway," said the neighbor.

Not in his wildest dreams did that farmer ever think Ombra would grow into the 140-pound beast he was today.

Carolyn drove up to the bench and stopped the engine.

With a huge smile and a twinkle in his eye Augie greeted her with, "Hello, Carolyn. How's my love?"

"Your love is beautiful, waiting in the harbor for me. I'm fine too, dear," she laughed.

Ombra sat unamused, perhaps a little jealous of Augie's affection of Carolyn. Carolyn reached down to pet him and the dog turned his head away, more interested in watching a bee fly toward the nearby vines. He treated her with disinterest. Ever faithful to his master, Ombra only tolerated her presence. She couldn't help but note the air of skepticism in his attitude toward her.

Carolyn loved visiting with Augie. He was such a huge part of her present happiness. He'd spent endless days teaching her how to handle his love, the yacht, and they had become close friends. Almost family. He would tell wonderful tales for hours on end if she let him. He always included his favorite story of how he'd first sailed the Eleganza, quickly correcting himself, by adding, I mean The Kiss Goodnight.

"It's OK, dear. I know she will always be your Eleganza," Carolyn said.

They sat together in the shade of coral bougainvillea that draped from the trellis over the stone veranda. Huge earthenware pots anchored each post, holding up the structure. Ombra, Augie's ever-present shadow, sat at his heels.

Located to the west of the house, it allowed them to gaze out over row upon row of neatly planted vines and beyond to the sea. They'd solved all the world's problems while sitting here many an evening.

I hope that old Luca Benedetto didn't give you a hard time on the road, Carolyn. He's harmless, but such a menace!" Augie said.

"Who?" Carolyn asked.

"Luca Benedetto He's not quite right. But his folks are nice and he's never really done any harm. Just likes to chase folks on the road for some reason," he said. "Saw him drive by just before you got here."

Carolyn didn't answer, but feeling much relieved, she sat back and took a sip of wine.

"This is one of the most wonderful places I've ever been," she said.

Augie had treated Carolyn like a daughter from the first time they'd met. Always kind and thoughtful, he took the time to teach her about the things he loved: the land, sailing, and his wine. It wasn't long before she looked at him as the father she always wished she'd had.

They shared gossip from the harbor while enjoying a small glass of wine with a bite of hard parmigiana and peppery arugula atop a hunk of crusty bread.

"I'd like two bottles of Rossese Di Dolceacqua, Augie," she said, slowing pronouncing each syllable.

"And I need to get going. The morning is slipping away."

Augie laughed. "Better take four," he said. "Best wine in the country, if you ask me."

Scooting along the winding road back down to the village, she kept her eye out for Luca Benedetto as she smiled at her unwarranted caution.

I'm safe, she thought, shaking her head.

She made a quick stop at the baker for fresh bread before heading back to the yacht. She wanted to keep the grapes chilled before they warmed in the increasing heat of the day. Once the loot from the early morning outing was on the boat, she went fishing for dinner.

She hated killing the fish, but damn, they were so good.

Slipping through the water with just a snorkel and fins like an expert, she marveled at how her arms and legs had gained so much strength and muscle definition. Sailing and swimming had done more for her than the fancy health clubs or spas she used to frequent. She swirled her hair around in the water and closed her eyes.

She felt proud about how much she'd improved in the few months she'd been here. It'd been a hard cold winter in Maine, but she realized she'd needed that time to herself as much as she'd needed it to hide. Thinking of Sandy and Maine sent a shiver through her shoulders.

The water was crystal clear at the edge of the shallows where she liked to snorkel and spearfish. Tumbled boulders arranged themselves like haphazard stair steps making their descent into the ever-darkening aqua water.

Thirty feet below eels were resting in dancing sea grasses. Algae ranging in color from gold to dark green, with tufts of rust, waved on the rocks. Octopi and starfish preyed on the sea urchins attracted to an umbrella-shaped seaweed cleverly called Neptune's Shaving Brush.

Carolyn swam between the boulder alleyways and rocky crevices while watching seahorses play hide and seek as she startled small schools of skittering fish. Occasionally she would find a piece of smooth coral in the seabed. She would slip those little treasures into the foot of her flippers. Streaks of sunlight pierced into the clear water and bubbles from the waves did a once-over tumble before heading back to the surface.

She speared a large Branzino, one of her favorites. The meat of the Branzino is tender, like grouper, but meatier and with more flavor.

Luckily they swam in large schools. It made it so much easier. Even so, she was becoming a fine fisherman.

Yes, she was very pleased with herself. Her insurance check cleared, her house sold, and she'd transferred her savings account. For the first time in her life she felt comfortably well-off. She marveled at how different her life was as she cleaned and seasoned her catch.

Instead of her usual preparation, a simple squeeze of lemon, today she decided to prepare the fish with a thick salt coating. She'd learned this technique from the sweet little lady in the pastry shop who'd supplied the sweets for her naming ceremony. This method sealed in all the flavor and kept the fish moist while it baked. Carolyn thought she'd someday try this preparation for a special occasion.

She hoped tonight would become just that.

CHAPTER 5

With a few hours to kill before Griff arrived, Carolyn lay sunning on the lounge. The familiar weight of the gold and diamond chain from her brother comforted her as it dangled around her ankle. The exquisite piece of jewelry had three nice-sized diamonds set between each link. In contrast to the elegant chain, the heart-shaped clasp was unusually large, even gaudy. Probably to allow for the sentimental engraving: Open your heart ~ Look within.

The chain had been a great solace as she attempted to forget the horror of losing her brother. Her eyes moistened with familiar pain.

As the yacht lolled in a mesmerizing rhythm, it caused the diamonds to sparkle a shimmery code that all was well.

Light and shadow from creamy clouds marbling the sky danced across her body as she lifted her face to the sun. Sea gulls squabbled overhead as graceful Gannets dive-bombed into the smooth surface of the sea far out from shore. A deep purple shadow edged the horizon where a cormorant flew into that place where the sky and water meet. His wings flapped in slow motion as he faded from sight. She closed her eyes.

***

It wasn't long before Griff stepped aboard the yacht. He let out an admiring whistle when he noticed the restored teak.

At that moment, an inconsiderate powerboat buzzed past. Its wake caused the yacht to roll in the waves. Griff crouched down and spread out his arms in a surfer stance, looking around as if he were being attacked.

It was rude to leave such a large wake. And on top of that, the jerk still has his fenders down, splayed out like a giant water bug. Augie would've said having the fenders down while underway is as detestable as toilet paper hanging on your shoe!

The thought of Augie getting irate at improper sailor decorum made her grin.

"Oh my God, you're such a landlubber," Carolyn laughed with a squeaky voice she didn't like at all.

OK, settle down, she told herself. But as she chastised herself, she couldn't keep her eyes away from Griff's full pouty lips with the dip down the middle and his cute button nose. She thought about kissing him right then.

Griff's blue eyes crinkled as he threw back his head of thick, full hair and let out a hearty laugh.

"Come here, kitten," he said.

She loved his laugh. It was so genuine and full of mischief. And she loved the way he laughed at himself too, making himself the butt of many of his own jokes. That characteristic was a big factor in winning her over. He'd never tried to impress her with his important family or his money.

As she walked toward him, she followed his gaze. His eyes slipped over the roundness of her sculpted shoulders and continued on to the smooth softness of her collarbones before halting to linger at the hollow of her perfumed throat. She smiled and straitened her back feigning a boldness she didn't feel. She'd been second guessing wearing the plunging, off-the-shoulder sweater until his eyes lit up with the glow of a striking match and swept over her breasts like a flaming forest fire. Her long, loose slacks only fanned the flame as they flowed effortlessly with her slightest movement.

"Hello," she said shyly.

Her confidence had been all but lost for more than a year now.

Stolen! Not lost, she thought.

With a deep breath she tried to convince herself, once again, that the odds of running into another murdering psychopath were slim.

Courage, despite fear. That's what Mike always said. "The courage is in your heart. You only need to look within."

Carolyn's brunette hair shone in the sun as she lifted her chin and smiled her private thoughts.

She reminded herself that it was only a date.

Griff whistled again as he grasped her hips for a quick embrace. His fingertips lingered on the luxurious silk fabric of her slacks. Carolyn braced herself. His luscious lips parted and his kiss landed on the corner of her mouth with the dexterity of a broken-winged butterfly. He repositioned with a slow, sweet hello kiss and she felt her body shudder with excitement as his mouth passed lightly over hers.

The slight chafe of his beard against her face scratched deep below the surface of her desire. She closed her eyes. When she opened them, he was looking into her... beyond her eyes... into her soul. Her face warmed. In this heady trance, her life before him vanished like a long-suffering ghost released from its penitent imprisonment on earth.

His soft eyes, staring at her so serious now, sparked with a jade undercurrent of heat-lightning that flashed through his gaze with explicit unspoken words.

She took his hand and led him toward the stern. The large lounging and dining area surprised him.

"This reminds me of stories I've read from The Arabian Nights. You are Scheherazade, aren't you kitten?" he asked with a wink.

"I demand not only this night, but one thousand more!" he said as he swept his hand along the glossy lacquer finish of the large mahogany table in front of the lounging area.

Her yacht *was* stunning and at this moment she did feel like a princess in an exotic storybook. Although the many long hours spent on her hands and knees scrubbing and oiling the shining wood wasn't nearly as glamorous as standing on it in the moonlight now. It'd been hard work, but she'd enjoyed it. It'd been magic for her soul. It looked fantastic, and she was proud to give him the tour.

They could see Ramone, the dock boy who'd painted the

name on her yacht, reaching the dock. She'd arranged for him to drop Griff off on her yacht in the outer edge of the bay so they would be away from the busy harbor.

Ramone, the gangly, dark-haired young man from the marina, did all the chores the old salts were too uninterested or lazy to do. They could have never guessed how much money he was adding to his small bank account every week and that one day he would be in charge of the entire harbor and marina.

But now that they were alone, she found herself biting her lip and saying, "Um." She poured them each a glass of wine and they settled into the oversized white cushions of the lounge.

Griff's story, as he'd told it, started with him growing up on a barrier island off the coast of South Carolina. The son of a military man, he and his parents traveled the world before stationing in Charleston where his father eventually retired.

Surfing, painting, and chasing girls filled his youth and young adulthood, until one day he realized his ability to paint was a gift. He'd decided he should try to make the most of it by settling down and painting in earnest.

"I spent most of my life there until the divorce," Griff said.

He sat silent for a moment as his face grew sad.

"I did well for myself, I don't mind saying. My oil paintings of the low country marshes and moonlight hang on prestigious walls all over the world.

"I provided a good life for my wife, and while she was proud of my celebrity, such as it was, and content enough when times were flush, it wasn't what she'd wanted. She came from one of Charleston's old families, attended the finest schools, and was the belle of numerous cotillions in her youth.

"Her friends always looked down their noses at me. She loved nothing more than dressing up in fine gowns, dining at Charleston's finest restaurants, and throwing elegant parties. I dreaded the pretentious of it all.

"I was happy in cut-off jeans and a ripped painting shirt. Why, I'd rather ride my old bicycle along the surf at dawn and dusk, noting every nuance of color and light, than gab with the rich folks. The harder I tried to fit the image of what she wanted me to be, the harder it was.

"I found myself overweight, on antidepressants, and with no motivation whatsoever. And to top it off, no matter how hard I tried, she grew tired of my art, my lifestyle, and my obvious charm," he said with a smile.

Carolyn smiled back at him.

"After the divorce, I kicked around Charleston for a while until I realized she didn't want me back. Ever!"

He widened his eyes as if the thought were inconceivable. Carolyn tried not to smile.

"She moved on to one of those snobs who always wore a designer hanky in his sport coat pocket. Can you believe that? She's shittin' in high cotton now and it sticks in my craw like hair on a biscuit."

Carolyn giggled.

"So, after that, I flew to Paris and bummed around Europe for a while. The Louvre was my first stop. I'd always dreamed of seeing the great works of art in Europe and that was as good a time as any.

"Heartbroken and lonely, in the back of my mind, I realized this was actually the best thing that'd ever happened to me. I'm in great shape again, excited, and have a renewed passion for my art," he said as he jokingly flexed his arm in a muscle man pose.

Carolyn couldn't help but notice the forlorn look on his face as he sat staring into the sea as if mentally weighing the outcome.

"I was only in Portofino for two days when I met you, Carolyn. My next stop would have been Rome, but that's on the back burner for now."

He reached to hold her hand and then brought to his lips.

"Mm, nice," he said.

After a few quiet moments Griff said, "Are we going sailing, or what? Let's get this show on the road!"

"Aye Aye Captain," Carolyn said with a laugh as she pulled the anchor.

Griff reached out and pulled on the boom.

"I can help if you need me," he said, exaggerating a confused look.

"Just sit back and look pretty, darling. That's what you can do to help," she said as she pulled his hand from the line.

Griff sat back and watched her handle the yacht single handedly, shaking his head in amazement. The light of the moon framed her easy motions against the backdrop of the dark forested mountains edging into the sea. He didn't know most of the motor-sail Gulet's work was done mechanically.

Carolyn walked past Griff and ran her fingers through his whipping hair to smooth it. It surprised her that the action came so naturally.

Griff reached out his pouty lips in a kissing motion and she gave him a quick peck.

She actually felt happy.

The rigging took turns serenading them with hushed whispers and taut snapping's as they sailed north. The hull creaked and groaned drowning out the contented gurgling as the sea rushed past the bow.

They passed the tiny enclave of San Fruttuosa and headed toward to one of the secluded bays Augie had shown her in her first heavenly weeks on her yacht. She'd anchored here alone, sometimes for a week at a time, never seeing a soul. Now she wanted to share it with Griff.

As Carolyn passed in front of Griff, she noticed him eyeing her figure. Her long flowing slacks were very thin. It was easy to see through the sheer white fabric that she was toned and tan. Her breasts, held firm and high by a delightful miracle of design under the clingy sweater, accentuated her narrow waist. As Carolyn glided by, her movements brought to his mind the cadence of a beautiful poem. It brought to his body something firmer.

"Lawwdy Child, if those britches were any thinner, I'd be able to see your religion," Griff said with an uncomfortable laugh before he took a quick gasp and forced his gaze toward the moon.

"The full moon rising in July is called the Full Buck moon. It's when deer get their new antlers," he said as he glanced at her slacks out of the corner of his eye.

"It's also called the thunder moon because it coincides with thunder from the many storms created in the summer."

He cleared his throat.

She tried to hide her smile while he nattered on about rising and bucking and thunder as she began to feel much more confident in her 'religious' slacks.

The silver light of this thunder-buck moon etched the mountains from the coastline before bathing the deck of The Kiss Goodnight in an otherworldly glow. A light breeze pawed at the sea's surface causing the yacht to rise and fall slightly as it sliced across the water.

Flecks of midnight shadowed the last remnants of daylight as a murder of crows flew off in a black scatter. Their raucous caws grew softer as they disappeared into darkness.

One lone crow flew in and perched on the clew of the boom. He nodded his head up and down as he perused the scene. His judgment came as a strident horsy rattle followed by a very loud clack. Then he flew off, his feathers gleaming like coal in the moonlight.

Carolyn hadn't been able to take her eyes off that crow. Somewhere, long ago, she remembered hearing that a squawking raven was the spirit of a murdered man. She wondered if it were the same for a crow.

Watching the crow made Carolyn feel uneasy. For whatever reason, she took it as a warning, a foreshadowing of doom. She turned around to Griff, hoping he hadn't noticed. A sassy crow had shaken her, and she knew it was silly. But Griff's gaze had settled on her bare shoulders.

"You smell of lavender and salt air," he whispered, his voice growing husky.

"I gathered a large basket of fresh lavender from a farm I visited during my travels around Provence before coming to Italy. I love the fragrance and tie sprigs of it under the showerhead," she said.

It was a faint scent. She was surprised he'd noticed.

Her lips turned up in an impish smile as she wondered if he'd smell of lavender soon.

As Griff drew Carolyn close, he pivoted her hips closer to his. The nubby fabric of his seersucker jacket brushed across her hands. He leaned in and kissed her. She kissed him back with an eagerness that surprised her.

The rest of the world faded into darkness as Griff's eyes conveyed what was coming next. His look of hunger evoked in her such a sudden yearning for consummation that her heart trembled.

She found herself powerless to turn away, had she wanted to. The impact was so strong that in that short span of time she knew this bond of intimacy would remain with her always.

Feeling faint, she turned her back to him. His eager lips kissed and nuzzled until they discovered her soft earlobe. A pleasant prickle covered her like a cool satin comforter under the light caress of his fingers skimming down the curve of her back. Her boldness astonished her again when her trembling arms reached around him.

He slid his hands down her shoulders as slowly as chilled butter melted on a lukewarm pancake. When he reached her fingers, he caressed them, entwined them with his own, and then held them to his face. He kissed each one as if it was part of a holy ceremony.

She loved the way he touched her. She loved the way he held and kissed her hands and she loved the way he was standing firm behind her. They stood silent for a long moment.

"Are you hungry?" she asked him, chastising herself at the same moment the words came out of her mouth.

"Yes, I'm starving," he said with a growl. She knew he wasn't talking about food.

She laughed while pulling away from him, knowing she'd ruined the moment. Her nervousness had shattered it. She headed toward the galley, pulling her shoulder length hair up into a loose bun. Maybe a cocktail would calm her nerves. She hadn't realized how much of her self-confidence she'd lost.

She emerged from the galley a few moments later balancing a silver tray with drinks and the large salt-crusted fish. A quick crack from the back edge of a heavy knife and the fish released a puff of steam, a hiss, and a savory aroma rivaling those from the fine harbor restaurants in Portofino. A squeeze of lemon finished it. Sliced tomatoes with fresh Mozzarella, basil, and a few ripe olives served as a salad. Crusty bread with fresh herb butter and the Rossese Di Dolceacqua wine completed the feast.

"Sweet darlin, this is so good, I would push my momma in a ditch if I could eat just one more bite," he said as he finished.

"But seriously, Carolyn. Deeeelicious."

"You're so silly!" Carolyn giggled.

His face became somber as he took another sip of wine. He watched her intently as the candlelight flickered shadows on her skin.

Her high cheekbones, soft delicate nose and perfect mouth, as she spoke every word mesmerized him with the smooth hypnotic charm of a King Cobra swaying out of a basket. She knew he was being seduced in the same way she was.

After dinner Griff stood at the deck rail with his glass of wine and looked out at the gentle waves capping white in the moonlight.

"The beauty of this day has frescoed the hard plaster walls of my heart. I will carry this memory with me forever. Thank you, Carolyn," he said.

Carolyn's pulse thrummed through her ears. She leaned her face against Griff's shoulder and their hands entwined.

"Over there, darlin'. There's more," Griff murmured, pointing to stars blossoming in the heavens like a giant bouquet of baby's breath. A pine freshness lingered on the light breeze wafting over them.

Griff turned and held her face in his hands as he leaned her back on the lounge. The gold and diamonds around her beautiful tanned ankle glimmered in the moonlight.

"This is where I'll begin," he said as he reached down and caressed her calf.

He kissed her slender ankle and teased his tongue toward her thigh. Her breath caught in her chest as she forced herself to breathe.

She had loved his playfulness and the way he made her laugh. And now she loved this, too.

"You are like spice to me," he whispered as he kissed her behind the knee.

"Most of the other women I've known were like a bloody Mary or a gumbo, in sore need of tabasco. Bland, no flavor, and definitely no heat."

"Umm, I love a good gumbo."

Carolyn woke three hours later to the mizzen halyard tapping monotonously against the mast. She blinked toward the blue glow seeping through the leafy branches as it etched the trees from darkness. As she lay there and let the moment sink in, a hint of sun prepared to embrace the cloudless sky.

It was a new day. New possibilities. A fresh page to be written.

Purple and green iridescence shimmered from the black wings of an elegant white stork. He stood still on his thin red legs, poised to skewer a breakfast delicacy with his pointed red beak. The fluffy white ruff of his neck and chest feathers matched the white plumage of his graceful head making for a very well dressed bird, indeed.

In contrast, a frumpy pelican, resembling an unfortunate-nosed bum that had slept in his faded brown suit, circled round and round before taking another dive. Coming up empty for the third time, he flew away hungry. Right on cue, the rock pipits and song thrushes began tuning up one by one before filling the trees with thousands of tiny songs just in time for their sunrise curtain call.

Griff walked to the railing and looked down into the clear water.

"Let's cool off. I'm hotter than a two-dollar pistol. Last one in has to make breakfast," he said.

You go ahead," she laughed. "I'll make breakfast."

Griff dove in and swam so deep, Carolyn lost sight of him. She pulled on a robe and went into the galley to start breakfast.

Two huge, hot and steaming Panini's, with fresh spinach, feta, tomatoes and fried eggs were waiting when he climbed back on the yacht.

"Um um! this is darn good, darlin'. I'm about as happy as an old porch dog," he said.

Carolyn chuckled as she headed to get in the shower first.

The soft pearl haze from the pale moon of last night drifted into oblivion as a liquid amber radiance spread out over the sea.

While Griff took his turn in the shower, Carolyn lifted the anchor.

She planned to keep him for a while. She'd stop at the market if he needed anything.

"Are we moving darlin'?" Griff shouted from below. I'm not ready to leave our cove just yet!"

Carolyn smiled.

CHAPTER 6

Every place on earth has a uniqueness that defines it. The landscape, the sky, the scent, the cities or towns, the mountains, rivers and the valleys… The people… Some places have a lyrical and romantic beauty that have attracted artists and writers throughout the ages for inspiration.

This coast of Italy was just such a place. And it was here, in this lovely timeless niche that Carolyn Wingate's life began again.

With Carolyn at the helm, they sailed past San Fruttuoso and agreed they'd made the right choice in continuing to head north to anchor. There was a buzz about the marina as divers from around the world were preparing for the annual dive to the Christ of the Abyss, a bronze statue of the Christ submerged off the coast. They both much preferred the solitude of their private cove.

She gave the wheel a smooth turn and steered out to the open sea heading for Corsica. She wanted to make love to him in France.

The power of the brisk wind moved them through the water as sea spray glistened her cheeks.

A few white puffs dotted the sky to the west in an otherwise cloudless sky. Nothing ahead but shades of blue stretching out forever.

Griff stepped behind Carolyn and nestled his chin between her shoulder and neck. A light morning haze hung just above the sea's face. Alone in the huge expanse of the mysterious sea, grinning with pure joy, they cut through each wave together as they cruised through the passage of time.

"Mmm, darlin'," Griff murmured as he brushed his face against her cheek.

When they spotted Corsica several hours later, Carolyn came about and followed around the cape heading south. A quilted backdrop of multicolored green framed the forested mountains around the quaint seaside towns dotting the coast.

They sailed on towards Calvi, a Corsican port most like the French Riviera. As they neared the town center, the cheery-colored stucco and terracotta tiled roofs gleamed a friendly hello. Palm trees lazily waved in the sun welcoming them to dock in the marina alongside beautiful multimillion-dollar yachts from all over the world. The Kiss Goodnight didn't look the least bit out of place considering her price tag was much less. Her classic beauty even made some of the big boys turn their heads occasionally.

Before hitting the grocery store for supplies, they stopped for lunch at a sidewalk café close to the harbor, and then took a stroll around the busy town center. Tourist season was in full swing already, giving the town a lively vibe. Even in the early afternoon, the Chanel and Hermes crowd sipped fancy cocktails that graced the outdoor tables at trendy seaside nightclubs.

After they'd picked up groceries and a few miscellaneous boat items, Carolyn took Griff's hand and they headed back toward the marina. She didn't need to say anything. He felt the same way.

While they'd enjoyed the colorful atmosphere and shopping for a while, they both longed to get back to the boat to be alone with each other.

They slipped off the mooring lines and motored away from the dock. The weather was good, so they sailed half way down the coast of Corsica toward Bonifacio before setting anchor.

Content and happy, Carolyn fell into a deep, much needed sleep.

Pft, pft, pft... The sound reached into her subconscious with a bitter sweetness that made her groan. She opened her eyes to icy pings of rain pelting her skin. Swollen drops fell from the sky plunking on the canopy like the big pungent balls on the old black walnut tree over the hill where she grew up.

While they'd been sleeping, a storm front rolled in carrying frigid air and rain. Clouds raced across the sky in a whipped frenzy, writhing and churling with charged energy. The wind snapped at the flaps of the lounge cover.

"I didn't see this coming when I checked earlier," she shouted over the wind. "Damn! Help me get this covered," she said.

"Lead the way, Captain. Guess I'm not dead wood after all," Griff replied.

Griff stood on the opposite side of the cushioned lounge, mimicked her moves, just a step behind, and helped her unfurl the canopy to cover it. The pleasant smell of petrichor that frequently accompanies rain after a dry spell drifted from the nearby rocky cliffs.

"This looks like it might be a real frog wash kitten," Griff said.

Carolyn giggled as she wondered if all southerners say such funny things or if she'd just found herself a special one.

With the lounge covered, they headed inside. This was Griff's first time in the galley. Carolyn had redesigned the living area shortly after buying the yacht. She added tufted-leather swivel chairs where the dining area had been. The teak inside was finished as nicely as the exterior, giving it a sophisticated Old World feel. The furniture, covered in the finest Italian leather, gave it a rich and earthy ambience with the rugged musky smell of new leather. The counters and coffee tables had been custom made in Turkey by fine stone craftsmen.

Carolyn tossed Griff a thick Turkish towel as claps of thunder rolled across the darkening sky. Rain clinked against the glass panes with the dulcet tones of champagne flutes as freshly washed sea air rushed in through the cracked-open galley window.

"I love the energy of a storm," she said as she made Griff a cup of hot tea. "It's the charging ions or particles, I think," she said as she reached under the sink for the bottle of bourbon she'd found at an international shop somewhere. She added a splash and took it to Griff.

After lighting a few candles, she slipped into a long blood-red silk caftan she'd bought in Paris. She smiled remembering the purchase. The funny saleslady insisted she buy it even though she remembered thinking at the time she'd never wear it.

After applying a perfectly matched deep-red lipstick to her bow-shaped lips, she tousled her dark shoulder-length hair and walked into the parlor.

Griff looked up in surprise. He'd been sitting in one of the leather chairs sipping bourbon tea, admiring the room, and enjoying the leather's softness and aroma. The Artsy-looking weather devices had caught his attention as the floating colored orbs bobbed up and down in the blown glass.

"This is nice," he said as he brushed his toes across the luxurious Turkish carpet. "Very masculine. Not like the pretty veils on the canvas, this is warm and sensuous.

"Each square on the rug has a different flower from the provinces in Turkey," she said.

"This is a place you could do some deep thinking," he said. "I love it. It couldn't have been better if it had been designed strictly for a man."

"I designed it for myself. It's where *I* like to think. And this is the only place I feel safe," she said, not at all surprised by his comment. Having worked in construction most of her life, she was familiar with men holding tight certain facets of what was considered manly.

The soft silk of her blood-red caftan glided over his leg as she brushed by him. Carolyn took a sip of Bourbon, no tea, and sat on the carpet near his feet. She took another sip of Bourbon, draped the soft caftan around his thighs, and opened her deep red lips.

CHAPTER 7

"The essential thing is to spring forth, to express the bolt of lightning one senses upon contact with a thing. The function of the artist is not to translate an observation but to express the shock of the object on his nature; the shock, with the original reaction.

-Henri Matisse

It's long been said that the ragged crags and smooth linen sands of southwest Corsica inspired Henri Matisse to master the expressiveness and emotion of color. Carolyn now understood why.

The mistral winds blowing from the northwest affecting the eastern Mediterranean on the coast of France from Marseille to St. Tropez were responsible for the exceptional sunny conditions and the desert-like vegetation in this charming and relatively undiscovered part of the French Riviera. A place Carolyn and Griff were beginning to think of as theirs alone.

Griff laid back on the lounge, pulled a thick white pillow under his neck, and closed his eyes.

"That wind sure is somethin'," he said.

"It's the mistral," Carolyn said. "Usually sweeps the coast with pleasant breezes. Its dry cold air blows hard and evenly leaving the sky clear and tinged in that unbelievable shade of blue. But when the air piles too high and cold in the Alps, it spills over the mountains and rushes down the Rhone valley. Its steady howl sets most people on edge with restless sleep and uneasiness in the soul."

"Well, I know a thing or two about the wind too, darlin'," he said as he ran his hand through his blowing hair.

"It's makin' my hair feel cat chewed."

"You nut," she said trying to mimic his drawl.

They continued to sail south along the coast toward the Strait of Bonifacio, passing small enclaves perched high on cliffs overlooking the coast. Mostly hidden in the trees, the terra cotta roofs gave them away by gleaming in the sun.

As they curved around the heavily wooded bluff, a low mass of limestone outcropping gathered at its base caught Carolyn's eye. The rocks looked desperate, as if grasping to flee the sea, as wind gusts rolled waves over them.

Smaller boulders, strewn higher on the beachhead were victorious in their escape where they rested lazily and forever on slivers of beach ranging from white sand to black stones.

She subconsciously watched the waves, sensing the struggle of the rocks to be free of the sea. And the victory of feeling free even if only a few yards away. It reminded her of her escape that night in the canoe when Andrew sent that large man to kill her. She wondered if she were truly free. Or if freedom was even possible.

Griff sensed her uneasiness and squeezed her waist. As Carolyn turned and kissed his cheek she tried to convince herself she was fine.

The sun had been harsh and blinding all day, but as it began to set, wispy high clouds in the shape of cuttlefish bones appeared in the sky. Golden at first, they faded pink, and then charcoal.

"Help me fasten the stern warps and toss the fenders Honey. We're near the channel markers on the chart," she said.

Griff answered, "Aye, aye, Captain," as he headed to the stern.

"Ok. There's a red," she shouted as she turned the wheel.

The tall sandstone formations of the narrow cavern with cliffs on three sides appeared hand carved. Wind and rain from the north hollowed the tablet-like stacks of stone over the centuries into the perfect harbor. The cliffs themselves blocked wind from the south, east and west.

Carolyn and Griff bobbed their heads between the historic architecture along the cliff tops to watching the channel markers as they entered the harbor.

A stout citadel perched atop one dramatic limestone cliff appeared to be teetering above Bonifacio to the north while dreamy vistas of Sardinia and pinpoint sailboats stretched to the south.

Carolyn and Griff were eager to get ashore again to join civilization for a short time. They motored The Kiss Goodnight into the dock, tied off, and hopped ashore to stretch their legs on solid ground, or solid dock at any rate. They needed to take a moment to steady themselves on land.

Festive, inviting shops lined the marina full of cheerful shoppers. They buzzed around in colorful shirts, sunhats, and expensive designer sunglasses, each looking more glamorous than the next. A narrow cobblestone street, worn smooth from countless footsteps over the centuries welcomed them as they stepped off the dock. They walked around the bay before heading up toward the market area to have lunch and explore the town above.

They chose a quaint waterside restaurant with a lovely view from their table of the harbor and The Kiss Goodnight. The yacht looked innocent enough, keeping her secrets to herself while champing at the bit to get back onto open water. She loved being out and away from the confines of the close quarters of a dock. She preferred to run free and easy with the wind on her back and her mistress at the helm. But she waited patiently.

The dim light inside the restaurant evoked a cozy, seductive feel. Its dark wooden fixtures and sailing memorabilia from centuries past resembled the inside of a large old pirate ship.

The earthy aroma of salumi that hung from the hooks around the wine bar and a mild tinge of wood-barreled spirits complemented the ambiance. After the waitress seated them on the outside deck, they ordered a rustic charcuterie plate and a splash of Corsican wine.

The sun warmed Carolyn's face as she gazed out over the lapis lazuli bay. For some reason, the thought of that cold Maine winter last year and the death of her friend Sandy crossed her mind. She closed her eyes and let the heat warm her cheeks while she breathed in deeply all the marina and restaurant aromas until her calm returned.

She'd always been able to go 'gray rock,' a learned survival method as a result of her childhood. It was her way of dealing with whatever drama and idiocy were happening around her. She would just imagine herself as a gray rock. Nothing could affect her then. Nothing could get in. That worked fine until the death of her brother. At that point her rock cracked into a million pieces and then blew away in the wind.

She subconsciously learned a new skill to cope with drama and pain. When things got rough now, she ran. She would run until she found a place where things were smooth. She took a deep breath and sighed again. This place was smooth.

"Be right back, darlin,'" Griff said as he bent to kiss her forehead. "Gotta use the throne."

After a few minutes, Carolyn thought she heard Griff's voice. She leaned around the railing and saw him talking on the phone.

Carolyn wondered who he was talking to.

Her inquisitiveness must have registered on her face as Griff held up his finger in a 'wait a second' gesture.

Carolyn was buttering a crust of bread when Griff rushed back to the table.

"Just a man about a commission work," he said, "It was supposed to be finished by now."

Carolyn caught a fleeting hardness in Griff's face before he forced a weak smile and busied himself forking cheese and meat to his plate. He ate in silence with his shoulders slumped stiff for a few minutes before the tension dissipated and his usual smile returned to his face.

"I told him I was followin' my muse. I didn't mention the other stuff I was doin' with her," he laughed.

After lunch Carolyn held Griff's hand as they headed toward *Haute Ville*, as people often call the citadel's upper main town. Most of the townspeople lived behind the fortress walls in houses built over the centuries.

As they passed under the weathered metalworking of the drawbridge, Carolyn felt a weird sensation, an uneasiness. She slowed her step, glanced down the stone walkway, and then back toward the harbor.

This was the same sensation she'd felt when that silly crow

cawed from the boom the first evening Griff stayed aboard the yacht.

It was the sense of foreboding.

She shook her head to scatter the feeling and locked elbows with Griff. After turning once more to look back, they strolled arm in arm through the narrow winding streets of mustard-hued stucco houses.

The high walls of the houses themselves turned into barricades guarding the inside of the city with as much fortitude as the citadel walls guarded the outside.

The views between the houses took turns opening onto breath-taking vistas across the cliffs and out to sea or inland across the steep bluffs covered in fragrant maquis.

"They say once the aroma has been experienced, like the island itself, it is never forgotten," Carolyn told Griff.

Griff was fascinated as Carolyn shared that throughout history the maquis had offered ideal cover for bandits and guerrillas seeking shelter from authorities. The word maquis even came to mean armed resistance fighter during the French Resistance of the Vichy regime.

"I wonder if they used it for love. Now is as good a time as any to see if it would work. What do you say? There's plenty of cover. A quick dalliance?" Griff teased.

Carolyn squeezed his hand.

"No, not now," she said, but in her mind they were already making the most passionate love in between the narrow ridges of the fortress.

They wandered out of a narrow street onto a white sandy path that led away from the village to a distant bluff overlook. The heady fragrance of the flowering thicket, made even more fragrant by the heat of the sun, surrounded them.

Griff looked around, sat down on a soft sandy stretch, and reached out his arm to help her sit beside him. This island had mesmerized them both since they first spotted its dark silhouette emerging from the sea.

"I can see the whole world from up here," Griff said. "Or the only part I care about, anyway," he said as he brushed aside some tall grass so she could sit.

In search of the sweet nectar of the flowering maquis, a bee took landing on Carolyn's shoulder. Griff reached to swat it away, and while glancing at her face, noticed that in the shade of her hat, her eyes were the exact color of the sea behind her. Caught off guard, he looked shaken.

"Your eyes," he muttered.

Carolyn smiled as she leaned in to kiss him.

A rustle in the thicket caused them both to turn. Carolyn's eyes widened as her eyes darted through the brush looking for an escape or a rock for defense.

Her nose wrinkled and her face twisted in a grimace as she glanced over the bluff. It was a long way down.

A small herd of goats munching and frolicking in a merry hubbub bounded toward them. The leader of the small herd walked up to Griff, sniffed him with an impertinent, no-nonsense seriousness, and plopped down next to him. Apparently this was their spot to rest and take in the view.

Carolyn was still reaching for the rock when Griff took her hand.

"You're a might jumpy today. I reckon we best get along anyway, kitten. The smell of this fella could put a buzzard off a gut wagon," he said, pointing his thumb toward the head goat.

Still feeling rattled, Carolyn looked back as she held her nose and followed Griff.

With a turn around one high wall, they were back inside the village. As they admired the window dressings in the shops, they came upon a small art museum. Griff pulled her into the entrance with the excitement of a child. The museum building's architecture, ancient stone and rock, was as interesting as the art it housed. The sign at the ticket desk said the small antiquated establishment held the largest collection of Italian art outside of the Louvre.

Griff grew more and more animated wandering through the tiny rooms as afternoon became evening. As he explained, in the minutest detail, the different aspects of each painting and artist, Carolyn's eyes glazed over. She kept shaking her head in agreement deciding to just listen and enjoy his exuberance.

When they came to the end of the exhibit, Griff looked surprised and then disappointed. He took one last look back and nodded his head.

THE KISS GOODNIGHT

"I have an eye for art too, you know," she said. "But I buy my paint at the hardware store instead of the artist's supply boutiques, she laughed.

"Come on, my little painter. One more stop," Griff said as he pulled her toward the hand-carved steps.

"Legend says the 187 steep steps from the fortress to the sea were carved in a single night by Aragonese troops during an ancient siege," Griff said. "Read it on the menu at the restaurant."

"A great crew," Carolyn laughed, jokingly, as they climbed down a few steps.

The sunset glowed on the cliffs turning them from creamy golden to a blazing bronze.

"I ordered this just for us," Griff said as he waved his arm across the scene.

He leaned behind her, holding the side of the rock wall on either side of her waist and nuzzled her neck like he did when they sailed.

"Mm. I love that," she whispered.

As he brought her hand to his face for a kiss, they realized they were casting long spooky shadows on the glowing rocks below.

"Hey," she said. "I just remembered. This was the very place where the legends of giants in Homer's Odyssey were born. While Odysseus passed by this island on his way from Troy, he reported the man-eating giants, the Lystragonians, inhabited it."

Carolyn waved her arms, making monster shadows and pretending to attack Griff. Griff was more than happy to attack back. They played with the shadows of themselves until the light faded.

Griff pulled Carolyn to him and held his arms around her as they watched the city buildings below light up one by one.

Carolyn couldn't put her finger on it, but she felt eyes on her, as if she were being watched again. Even though they'd had a wonderful day, she hadn't been able to shake the strange sensation she'd had since lunch.

She'd told herself it was silly, but turned around a few times to check if anyone were following her. And she had it now, stronger than ever, as they climbed back from the steps.

She glanced behind her as they walked back down the ancient street toward the marina.

The sound of their shoes clicking and clacking on the ancient cobblestone streets echoed with the sound of wind and waves dashing against the cliff walls. The music and laughter in the village where locals had gathered to dance grew louder as they drew near. Carolyn felt relieved when they'd reached the lights of the café and shops.

The smell of fresh bread baking in the bakery and the fragrant maquis blowing from the cliff mixed with the smell of the local cuisine pouring out of every restaurant through the open doors.

"I'm starving!" Carolyn announced.

"I'm in full agreement, darlin'. Let's get you fed," Griff answered.

"Oh, am I the only hungry one?" she laughed.

They stopped in the same café where they'd had lunch and ordered a pizza and a bottle of Corse Figari Rose wine. The waiter advised that its pungent nose of herbal scents would go nicely with the goat cheese and sausage pizza they'd ordered.

"Corsica, King of Salumi?" asked Griff while reading the waiter's apron.

"Guess you'll have to be satisfied with the mere prince of salami while here in Corsica, darlin'."

Carolyn groaned.

When their food arrived, they devoured the pizza and wine and ordered an enormous lemon-flavored cookie to take back to the boat for breakfast.

She felt a sense of well-being she hadn't felt all day as they headed toward the boat.

Probably because of the great day adventuring, but the wine had helped.

"Mm. What a wonderful day," she said the Griff as they steeped aboard The Kiss Goodnight.

The instant she stepped below deck, the hair on the back of her neck stood up and goose bumps prickled her arms. She stood stiff while her eyes darted around the room. Everything looked the same as they'd left it.

But there was a tinge, or a hint of an aroma, a subconscious acknowledgement in her senses. It wasn't anything she could name, but she could feel it. It was on the tip of her awareness, just beyond her mind's grasp.

She'd felt uneasy off and on all day and now she was sure it was more than just her imagination. Maybe a lingering scent? Cedar and lemon? The memory of a glass pyramid-shaped bottle of cologne on a golden tray, the only item on Andrew's perfect dresser shot through her mind.

"Gold, frankincense and myrrh, the rarest and most expensive bottle of cologne in the world."

Andrews's voice sounded in her mind.

"A gift befitting the son of god, from an equal. From me to me," he'd said with his blaring, phony guffaw.

Carolyn shook. Those old feelings, almost forgotten, resurfaced with a vengeance.

I: Insignificant… Inadequate… Inferior…

All of these self-deprecating insults entered her mind with the vision of Andrew's face.

Griff, unaware of her sudden alarm, turned the radio to the weather channel. He was eager to set sail early and be off to the next port. He settled into the big leather chair and patted his leg. He wanted her near him. As she inched toward him, not saying a word, he frowned. She knew he'd noticed her anxiety. He held her on his lap and rubbed her arms in that comfortable way you do when you've been together for a long time, feeling like you're part of each other. She said nothing because she couldn't put into words what she was feeling without getting into the entire dreadful story.

"Let's sleep below tonight. Ok?" Carolyn asked. "I'm tired from hiking and the wine and need to get some sleep."

"Fine by me. Too noisy and crowded up here," Griff answered.

When Carolyn finished her shower, Griff told her he'd taken a turn around the deck to make sure everything was locked.

"I checked every room and closet and under every bed," he said after apparently noticing her uneasiness.

As she tried to get comfortable, she thought about the small pistol she'd hidden in the flooring under the sink in the galley. It calmed her to know it was there.

This was a safe and busy harbor. She told herself it was silly to feel this way. She was far away from her old life. Very far away. She wasn't in danger here. She was falling in love and happy for the first time in a very long time.

But her mind drifted again to the phantom gray 9mm under the floorboard. After a quick trip around the yacht to double check, Carolyn snuggled into Griff's arms and faced the window to the night sky. She loved the softness of Griff's hairy chest and the smell of fresh sandalwood soap as he snuggled her tight.

She watched the stars glitter in the dark and thought about the sunny bluff and the goats and the long scary shadows until she fell into a sound and much needed sleep.

CHAPTER 8

    Carolyn woke to an agonizing groan emanating from the dark place in her mind. She was running through the dark hallways of a large, ancient castle with heavy wooden doors and cold stone floors.

    The eerily incandescent fangs of two monstrous gargoyles glinted as they gaped open their dank, black mouths. Oozing gobs of gelatinous phlegm dripped between the strange blue glow of their razor-sharp teeth.

    They thrashed their tails, pounced over her, clicking their beastly jaws as they stretched their giant mandibles to engulf her face in their heinous breath. Their fur, what was left of it, was tufty and thin. Rancid scabs were rapidly replacing the pallid skin on their underbellies.

    Carolyn ran from one room to the next, hiding behind the long thick velvet curtains that the castles of nightmares always had. The monsters would find her, sniff, and scratch at the curtains with blood-caked claws, snarling until she ran along the scratched walls to the next room of the unending hall.

    As her world rushed by in a blur, Carolyn's foot caught, and in those few seconds suspended in the air, she prepared herself for impact.

    The red-yellow sparks in the gargoyle's eyes, the snake-like flicking of their tongues, and guttural growls were the last thing she saw before her head bounced against the cold stone floor.

    Carolyn winced at their hot expulsion of breath as the beasts prepared to seize her neck.

The door creaked and they froze still.

"Dracula! Renfield!" Andrew commanded.

He made a hand motion and the gargoyles heeled at his side. Carolyn looked up.

Andrew's straight light hair was thinner than she remembered.

By his side, he held a gnarled wooden cane with an engraved animal head and he wore a thick woolen sweater, corduroy slacks, and expensive-looking slippers.

Castle-wear, she subconsciously thought.

He also wore that stern sneer he always wore when he was displeased.

Carolyn woke with a start.

"It's him," she whispered.

She'd had the lingering presence of him in her mind from yesterday. It'd set her on edge when they came back from town. She smelled him. Or rather, a scent that reminded her of him.

Of course he hadn't been there. He has no idea where she was and certainly couldn't find her in the middle of the Mediterranean.

But still...

A cold shiver ran through her. She tried to put Andrew and the dream out of her mind. She wanted nothing from her horrible past to taint what she had now. She'd walked away from that other life, or more accurately, she'd run from it. It couldn't touch her now. She was safe. She was happy.

"Very happy," she whispered.

Carolyn shook her head as if to shake the demon and gargoyles from her brain just as Griff reached over to put his arm around her.

His eyes drifted open and a few minutes later Carolyn had rousted him from bed and they were on their way shopping.

They'd made a quick trip to get provisions before slipping the mooring line and setting sail for the east coast of Sardinia. Carolyn wanted to see the Bue Marino caves, supposedly the best caves on the island.

"According to the stories, the rare black Mediterranean seals used to give birth to their pups in the caves. The seals were gone now, but there are hieroglyphics from the ancient people that once inhabited the island I want to see," she said.

The mistral wind caused high seas to funnel with a fierceness between Corsica and Sardinia, making for quite a difficult sail. Once outside the mile-long inlet of Bonifacio, the sailing went swift and smooth as long as Carolyn paid rapt attention and stayed in the channel. The Mistral wind was known to play havoc with the currents in the strait as well as with your peace of mind. And Carolyn's peace of mind was hanging by a thread.

It was the wind, she thought. *Just the wind.*

Soon they found themselves sailing easily along the east coast of Sardinia. Stunning natural landscapes of high cliffs and narrow dark gorges framed the endless azure sky.

Thick unspoiled forests accentuated the sharp jutting mountains. Off in the distance they spotted long stretches of white sand beach and gorgeous little coves secluded by cliff walls.

Carolyn watched Griff as his hair whipped in the wind. The sea was deep and had taken on an emerald tone that reflected in his eyes.

Despite her feeling of gloom, she felt the irresistible impulse to smile

CHAPTER 9

> The screech owl, screeching loud
> Puts the wretch that lies in woe
> In remembrance of the shroud
> 					-William Shakespeare

Eastern Coast of Sardinia

The wind's dulcet ballad rose and fell, sighing through the sails and riggings as the shadow of The Kiss Goodnight grew long. The isolated mountains of eroded limestone, pockmarked with caves, gnarled trees, and rock pinnacles moored themselves in the bluest waters of the Mediterranean.

A small tour boat rocking and rolling like a porpoise playing in the surf struggled near the gaping mouth of the Bue Marino cave. The driver turned it against the waves at a forty-five degree angle, trimmed the engine, and then darted toward Cala Gonone, the nearest coastal town.

He must have been on a strict schedule to get the tourists back in time for their dinner buffet.

She'd decided to anchor in a cove south of the caves off the coast of Del Gennargentu national park to make for easy exploring in the morning. Sheer, bleached limestone cliffs streaked with scorched yellow and smeared burnished brown dropped straight into the sea to afford no beachhead.

"This won't be a quick anchor drop," she said as Griff got busy laying warps ashore in the direction of the strong prevailing winds. She held her snorkel mask to her face and dove deep to find a suitable rock outcropping to attach the anchor.

After they rested, she noticed Griff's hair was getting lighter in these few days of constant sun and his silver temples were growing white. It was striking against his tanned skin.

I love stroking my fingers through your hair. It's becoming my favorite resting pose." She said as she sat with his head in her lap admiring the green sparkle in his blue eyes while he looked out into the last of the flaming red and peach sunset.

"We worked hard today, she said. I'm beat! It was no easy task to sail away from Corsica."

Griff responded by closing him eyes and murmuring softly.

After a short rest, Carolyn busied herself by preparing blackened shrimp with wild herb and pine nut rice on the grill.

"I love the smell of this fresh cilantro I picked up at the market," she said as she added a small handful to the rice.

"That smells mighty good," Griff said as he swallowed the last of his large glass of lemonade. "I'm starving."

He reached around and kissed her just as terrible shrieking noise came from the dark woods along the cliff top. A chill ran down Carolyn's spine.

By the dim light of the moon they watched an owl smoothly glide across the face of the cliff, flare his wings, extend his claws, hover for a moment, then swerve to snatch up a small animal. Griff returned his attention to kissing Carolyn. And while she had a sharp chill running up her spine, she was warming to him again.

The owl's eerie warning screeched in her thoughts every time Carolyn closed her eyes that night. The wind blew in hard from the west to whip the waves in whitecaps before dashing away to make way for the next onslaught. Their anchorage held firm, but she felt haunted and tossed.

Dawn begrudgingly awoke with the same sense of gloom that Carolyn did. Heavy dark clouds covered most of the sky with a few shafts of silver light piercing through to stab at the sea. A family of wild boars snuffling around the top of the nearby cliff looked for roots and grubs, or maybe even ground bird eggs. A pair of honey buzzards soared above, calling to each other with their plaintive 'Peeee-luu' call.

Waking up with dread was a familiar feeling from long ago. She hoped her uneasiness was only the lingering nightmare.

After a quick breakfast they took the dinghy around the short distance to the gaping snaggle-toothed mouth of the cave.

Because of the overcast sky and choppy waves they were the only tourists to arrive this morning. The tourist boat from Cala Gonone would probably arrive midafternoon after the tourists had their fill of their all-inclusive breakfast and a morning swim in their ocean-side pool.

The old guide begrudgingly put out his cigarette and got up out of his old lawn chair. He told them to climb up to the wooden platform from their dinghy. He didn't appear too interested in taking two lone tourists back through the cave

"I already had that part figured out," Carolyn said under her breath, hoping he hadn't heard her.

Boy, I'm in a mood today, she thought, and shook her head. *Get over it.*

Because he wasn't going to bother taking them on the tour, the guide calculated a generous tip, and then overcharged them an additional few euros for having to make the effort in math. His tour consisted of telling them to walk along the trail to the sign that says turn around, be careful not to fall in, the bats wouldn't hurt them, and not to bother trying to open any doors to the off-limit sections of the cave.

"Is that what price the sign says?" Griff asked Carolyn. "I'm thinking that's not right."

"It's fine, darling. We'll have the place to ourselves," she said with a wink.

She was happy the old geezer wouldn't be escorting them.

After Griff paid, they walked over the fly bridge leading from the platform into the cave. A steep step from the wooden bridge led to the slippery rock path, worn smooth and slick by dampness and the many footsteps over the years. The sea inside the mountain was one of the largest cave lakes in the world, measuring more than a half-mile wide.

Color, from paper white to ink black with tarnished copper highlights, reflected against the stalactites and stalagmites onto the mirror-smooth water. As they entered deeper, the cave got darker. Old, rusted string lights with yellow bulbs hung every ten feet or so. It was enough light to navigate, but not enough to eliminate the creepy feeling that a slimy creature would reach out and touch you at any moment.

Carolyn walked behind Griff choosing her steps with care. They'd already passed the sign indicating the turnaround at end of the tour. Beyond that point darkness swallowed everything.

"Keep going," she whispered. I want to see the ancient hieroglyph drawings in the off-limits end of the cave."

That was another reason she was happy the guide was lazy today.

"Easy for you to say," Griff said softly. "I'm in front."

A soft drip echoed in the stillness from unseen spires deep inside the cool, humid cavern. Drip, drip, drip, the sound beckoned a macabre invitation into the unknown void.

"What was that?" Carolyn gasped.

She listened.

Her breath slowed as she tried to take in less of the damp, stale air.

Someone could've been right next to her and she'd never know.

Her hand reached into the darkness to the ageless damp stone of the rugged wall. She felt claustrophobic.

A slick, black rubber-gloved hand rippled the smooth surface of the silent, deep water. With a quick, silent pull, it gripped Carolyn's ankle. In the brief struggle her ankle chain broke and fell to the damp rock.

Before she could cry out, she was under water.

"Griff! Griff!" her mind screamed.

Yanked along underwater by her ankle, her captor came to a small hole in the wall. He grabbed her hair and pushed her through.

When her face broke the surface, she took a quick gasp. Jerked by her arm this time, someone dragged her under the water to another opening. Carolyn surfaced again. This time she used what breath she had left to scream. A thick rubber glove pushed her face and jerked her under water again.

Deep, deep, down they plunged.

When her assailant slowed, she floated toward him and eased close to the light bobbing around on his head. Salt water burned her eyes as she widened them in an effort to see who was doing this to her. Between the black diving hood and the goggles, she couldn't see anything that would identify him.

The slender beam of his head light flashed against the cave wall. Carolyn wedged herself between her captor and the cave wall and gripped his arm. She gave a quick kick to his face. She pulled back and kicked again with all her strength. He let go.

She kicked fast as she could to reach the surface.

This was nothing like she'd imagined when she realized she was about to die. She wasn't sure what she thought it'd be like. But this wasn't it.

Just when she thought her lungs would burst, her head broke the surface. Her deep gasps echoed in the cave like the screams of an alien being. It hurt her throat to breathe so hard. Panic shot through her as she opened her eyes to complete darkness.

Not sure it was possible to be frightened any more than she was, her gaspy screams echoed back to her and frightened her to the bone. Over her desperate splashing and gasping she heard herself whimper. It was a sound she'd heard from herself before. A sound she despised. She stopped it immediately.

Like dour notes of an untuned cello, drips plonked from the ceiling with the steady tempo of someone counting down her demise.

Carolyn floated in the total darkness and reached for anything to hold.

Her knee bumped into a solid form. With her arms stretched upward, she felt a smooth, flat space at the top. She hoisted herself out of the chilly water. The uncomfortable perch allowed her enough rest to recover her breath.

A few minutes before, it took everything within her to survive. Now out of the immediate danger of drowning, she realized her terrifying situation. She lay there not daring to move.

When she recovered her breath, she wiggled a few fingers

around the edge of the rock. Feeling braver, she moved her hands back and forth to get her bearings. She felt another rock. The thought of crawling to the next rock entered her mind. But then what? There was no light in this cave. That meant there was no way out. Except the way she'd come.

She knew she should swim back the way she came. But which way was that? She wondered if he was still here, while thinking he must have given up by now. Surely he would think she drowned. He'd know people would be looking for her.

Carolyn tried to remember what she'd read about the caves, but her mind was numb with fear. She would visualize the pictures she'd seen on the Internet, and then everything would fade.

"Breathe!" she told herself.

After a few slow breaths with her eyes closed, she remembered the caves had underground rivers running through them. That was how someone had pulled her to this secluded spot.

The river should flow out to the sea. Right?

Her next thought was a fuzzy one about deep breaths and a limited amount of oxygen.

She hunched down the side of the stalagmite and dangled her foot to see if she could feel a current.

"I feel it," she said to herself, her voice sounding hollow in her ears.

Carolyn's sense of direction had always been terrible so she wasn't sure if it was the way she had come or not. Add the total darkness to that, and who knew? Her leg dangled in the water, feeling for the current for what seemed like a long time.

"Steady nerves," she told herself, knowing she had to get her oxygen level at the highest before attempting to go back under water.

Slow, deep, purposeful breaths helped calm her down while adding oxygen to her blood. She began breathing deeper at closer intervals.

How long was I under? she wondered. *I can hold her breath for three minutes plus a few odd seconds. I came close to my limit with the first drag.*

The thought of it made her pulse jump.

Ok, back to steady breathing. No distractions now. I'll think about what happened, and why, later.

Carolyn lowered herself into the water and tread in the

direction she felt the current moving. She stopped every few feet to make sure she was following it. She floated with it for a minute or so.

The current, swifter now, ran her into a wall. She slid her foot along the slimy surface to feel for an opening. Just below her feet she felt a huge pull.

She took a deep breath and dove, following the current as it pushed through a narrow opening then into a tunnel. Her fingers felt raw as she pulled along the cave ceiling in the dark. The current moved faster, pushing her straight into the end of the tunnel. The water moved to the right, so she pushed off hard. She was running out of air. As she passed out of the tunnel, she kicked with every bit of strength she had. She worked her arms like never before and headed upward, hopefully into air. She gasped as she reached the surface.

Ok. Ok. That wasn't so bad, she told herself. It was the darkness that unsettled her. Maybe if she could see.

She tried to steady her breathing again.

Compose… compose, the words ran on a loop that overtook every other thought.

She tread water again until she felt the current. She followed the same pattern as before, stopping, feeling for the current before continuing. She passed through an opening that touched her head.

As she kicked her feet, she noticed the water was a mixture of warm ocean water and cooler river water. She knew she must be closer to the ocean.

The current floated her into another wall. She couldn't feel an opening, but she could feel that the current was strong below. Taking another deep breath she dove down, kicking hard again. She pulled herself along the wall deeper and deeper. She felt a blast of warm water and pushed herself through it. Now she was in the warmer water of the ocean. She swam to the surface, kicking as hard as she could. She saw light. And then she saw Griff.

He looked beside himself with worry. As soon as he saw her surface, he let out a deep groan and dove in to help.

An organized speleologist excursion planned for that afternoon had arrived early. It seemed a coincidence but there were cave diving groups that frequented here every other day. Just yesterday Griff had talked about diving with them.

Three of them stood where Carolyn had fallen. One diver's huge underwater flashlight cast maniacal shadows on the walls, making the scene all the more surreal. Two divers, already in the water looking for her, had their lights cutting through the darkness. The diver with the crazy flashlight caught a bright object in his beam on the rock path. It was her ankle bracelet. The clasp was broken.

"Carolyn, Carolyn, Oh my god! What happened?" Griff cried.

Stunned, everyone started yelling and clapping and I'll be damning. Once they'd pulled her to the path, Griff reached all the way around her and held her tight. Carolyn was in a state of shock and just beginning to comprehend what had happened. She stood shaking.

Someone from the diving group wrapped a jacket around her shoulders. The diver with the crazy flashlight was now shining it into the small crowd, telling them to back up. He edged over to her and handed her the broken chain. They all moved toward the entrance of the cave chattering with excitement. By this time the tourists had arrived and were filling the cave to hear about the drama.

Once on the platform, the old guide sat her in his lawn chair, pulled out a flask, and told her to take a swig. The liquid burned and tasted lemony. Griff was on both knees next to her, rubbing her shoulder.

Griff wrapped his arms around her from the back of the chair, knelt to the ground, and closed his eyes.

"Oh my god," he mumbled repeatedly.

An official-looking speedboat roared up while the small crowd gathered around Carolyn. A tall dark-haired man hopped off the boat and looked around at the crowd. Before he'd made it to her chair, he'd scanned every face in the crowd.

The police had their share of adventure in this area, dealing with tourists in the caves and the large National Park just to the south. Summer adventurers were always coming to town getting themselves in trouble. People fell in the water at the cave all the time. But the crackling concern in the old guide's voice on the two-way radio must have suggested this was different.

The official, handsome in a dark, cold way, Carolyn supposed was a cop. Likely because of his mirrored sunglasses and authoritative walk. Even though he'd shaven earlier, his face showed the hint of a

Five o'clock shadow. As it turned out, he'd come from Rome just yesterday.

As he walked toward Carolyn, the hair on the back of his neck stood up. He could see that even though she was as green and wrangled as a bit of washed-up seaweed, her features were delicate and striking. The fear in her eyes was palpable as she looked up at him.

Her beauty had caught him off guard and he lost the rhythm of his determined gait for a hair of a second before he recovered without giving himself away. Carolyn knew he'd seen her fear, and that this wasn't just a case of her falling in and causing drama.

"Get the people back," he said to the old guide as he stooped to one knee to speak to her.

As reality tried to pry through Carolyn's brain she held her breath to avoid hyperventilating before slowly letting it out in a long controlled effort.

The fear sat quietly, deep down, igniting thoughts of terror with each beat of her heart. She tried to calm herself as the contortion in her stomach reached her throat as if an invisible hand were smothering her.

Fight! Fight!

She fought the urge to start screaming and never stop.

"Look within!" her brother's words came to her.

She closed her eyes.

Look within, she thought again and again. *Look within.*

She calmed and opened her eyes.

The realization of what'd happened was clear. She knew this wasn't a random attack. Someone had followed her. Targeted her. And she knew who it was. Yes, she was terrified. She didn't need to look through the crowd. She knew he wouldn't be there. He was a phantom, a monster, and every other horrible thing she could imagine.

Carolyn was still in shock as the officer introduced himself. She looked up at him and shook her head, catching just the last part.

"You can call me Tomas," he said.

After drying off somewhat, she gave a statement. It was short.

"I was walking, saw a hand, was pulled in, kicked the

assailant, and here I am," she said.

As soon as the words were out of her mouth, she regretted them.

She should've lied, she thought. She needed to get away, not sit here and make a report that wouldn't matter, dammit!

Tomas gave her a look that said he thought she knew more than she was saying. And that he knew she wouldn't tell him any more than she already had.

He jotted down a few quick notes, had her sign it, and told her he would like her to come to the police station in Cala Ganone the next day. She said she would, but she could tell he didn't believe her. More than likely, the mystery of what happened would follow her as she sailed away.

As her breathing became steady, she calmed down.

She needed to think. And to do that, she needed to get back to the yacht.

With a recharging deep sigh, she stood up, handed the diver's coat to the guide, and walked toward the dinghy.

She couldn't fall apart now, she told herself as her insides began to shake. She needed to get back to her safe haven.

Griff jumped in the dinghy and steadied it for Carolyn before they took off toward The Kiss Goodnight. By the time they were back on board, Carolyn was thoroughly exhausted and completely unnerved.

This was a nightmare and she'd just woken up.

Griff tried to hold her, but she was distant and cold. She wanted nothing from him. It was as if he didn't exist. Right now the only thing that existed to her was fear. She was trying to control it, but she knew she hadn't even begun to get a grip on it.

Griff cracked the door open as she took a shower because he didn't want to lose sight of her again, even for a moment. She knew he wanted to hold her and protect her. But she didn't care.

She needed space. She needed to think.

She slipped into a long black velvet robe with matching pants.

"Here's a cup o' hot tea, darlin'. With a splash of bourbon," Griff said.

"Thanks," Carolyn answered with a weak smile.

She lit a candle and sat in one of the club chairs with her legs pulled up under her. With the furry blanket wrapped around her shoulders she took a sip of tea. Then another. She stared at the candle.

"How delicate the flicker," she said as she sat staring at it wax and wane in the slightest movement of air. It meant something, but she couldn't think.

"I'm tired," she said.

Griff sat next to her in the other chair and reached to hold her hand.

"What can I do, darlin'?" he asked.

He sat patiently before slumping his shoulders and watched Carolyn stare into space.

After a long while, Carolyn looked at him. For the first time since she'd been pulled from the water, she saw the concern on his face. After taking the last sip of tea she took his hand.

"Let's go to bed," she said.

Carolyn leaned back against Griff and stared out the window. She tried to relax but as warm and comforting as he was, her hypervigilant was as active as it had been as a small child.

Normally every creak and thump on the yacht lulled her to sleep. But she was wired on high alert. And when Griff's breathing become rhythmic, Carolyn slipped from his arms.

She tiptoed to her hiding place under the sink, pulled out the pistol, and tucked it in the pocket of her robe. She knew there would be big fines if she were caught her with a firearm in Italian waters, but right now she was glad she'd taken the risk. Grabbing the fur blanket, she wrapped herself and headed to the lounge. Even her soul trembled as she pulled out the gun, rested it on her shaking knee, and pointed it out into the darkness.

She watched.

As a cold dawn broke over the ocean, the forest above the cliff came alive. Coils of mist wrapping around the gnarled tree roots climbed up to the shaggy headed treetops. Shadows and dark patches clung in the tree hollows as light tried to banish them by poking through the mist and blackness. Every tree bore the suspicion of hiding a ghoulish secret. The wind echoed a hollow wail, dying back to a faint hush now and then.

The sound of a motorboat heading her way woke her out of a half-sleep. Carolyn looked north toward the cave and saw a small police boat. She tucked the gun in her pocket and stood up to stretch. She was going to need strong coffee.

Tomas approached The Kiss Goodnight fast, at a forty-five degree angle with his bumper already down. He tossed his bow line at the same time he jumped aboard.

"Permission to come aboard," he stated, rather than asked. He scrutinized the boat as if he were looking for a clue.

What could he expect to find here? she wondered. Must just be what cops do. Mike was like that too. Always looking around. Always investigating.

Tomas continued eying the boat as he walked up to greet Carolyn. She invited him to sit down at the dining table and offered to get him coffee.

A private person by nature, Carolyn had become more private by instinct and experience over the years. The reason she'd purchased The Kiss Goodnight was to be unreachable. She didn't want Andrew to find her. Or anyone. That's why she ran away. She'd been through enough already and had hoped for some peace in her life.

Tomas took another look around, from bow to stern, before sitting down. The crease in his forehead indicated he sensed something hinky. He took off his mirrored sunglasses and looked her straight in the eye. His serious dark brown eyes were as hard to read as a pocket copy of a King James Bible through the tinted windows of a long black limousine.

Carolyn wasn't the only one who liked privacy.

Tomas knew Carolyn was withholding information about the incident in the cave. And he knew she wasn't just another American on holiday. Someone had reported her missing in the United States. A substantial reward for information on her whereabouts was posted in the United States, Europe, and Central America.

Carolyn knew nothing about it.

The report said she was the missing girlfriend of a very wealthy American. His family had immigrated to the United States in the 1800s. They'd become one of America's most prominent families by founding one of its most successful corporations. They'd also played a large part in politics in the eighteenth and nineteenth centuries.

What was widely known about the boyfriend in his rich American circles was that he'd accomplished little, other than living large off his trust fund. But Tomas knew much more than the grocery store rags and Internet gossip columns reported.

Carolyn excused herself and came back with two steaming cups of espresso. There was a shot of something extra in hers. She sipped the hot coffee and handed him his cup. She knew she would have to give him an explanation.

But what? How much did he need to know? How much did he already know?

Toma's brow furrowed and his chin cocked upward as he studied her face. The lashes on his dark brown eyes were so thick he appeared to be wearing eyeliner. His lips pursed into a thin line and a muscle in his cheek kept bobbing up and down as if he was clenching his teeth.

"What happened back there?" he asked.

"I thought someone grabbed my foot," she started, "but it might have all been my imagination. It was dark in that cave and it unnerved me. The creepiness of it all. I probably just slipped, panicked, and imagined it."

He looked at her, not wavering his eye contact. Carolyn knew he wasn't buying it.

"I apologize for causing so much trouble. I would like to pay for any expenses associated with the incident," she said, hoping that would do it.

Tomas kept staring at her.

"I know who you are," he said.

Carolyn's world suddenly became very small. A bolt of electricity shot through her. Her eyes widened. But before she could say anything, Griff came out of the galley carrying his own cup of espresso and a couple of cookies. Carolyn looked Tomas in the eye and shook her head no, beseeching him not to say anything.

It surprised Griff to see Tomas on board as he hadn't heard him arrive. He sat at the table with them eager to hear any update on the case. He cocked his head and hunched his shoulders when he heard there was no news. Then his eyes squinted toward Tomas, wondering what he was doing here then.

Tomas stood up to leave and handed Carolyn his card.

"If you need anything or have any questions, you can get hold of me. Otherwise, I'll see you tomorrow at the station. Right?" he asked.

He didn't know if she knew about the reward or not, but he didn't mention it.

"In the meantime, I have the radio frequency of your boat, I'll let you know if anything turns up," he said.

Carolyn finished her coffee as the small police boat headed around the cove out of sight. She bent to kiss Griff on the forehead, threw the business card overboard, and then headed below deck to get dressed.

Griff was still at the table enjoying his second cup of coffee when she came back and asked him if he had a particular destination in mind.

"If not, I'm planning to sail to Capo Carbonara on the southern coast of Sardinia to see the pink sand," she said.

Griff looked surprised. "I don't understand wanting to leave right away, darlin'," he said. "Shouldn't we wait to hear some news?"

Carolyn didn't answer.

CHAPTER 10

Pink granite rocks jutted from the highest point in Capo Carbonara promontory to overlook the Covoli and Serpentara islands. Masses of yellow tinged wild flowers softened the rocky hillsides along this eastern end of the Gulf of Cagliari.

As The Kiss Goodnight approached the tip of the island, they sailed past the Caribbean blue salt lake, separated from the shallow sea by a narrow bar of sparkling pink sand. Heat waves glimmered above the large shallow lagoon where a huge colony of pink flamingos called their favorite winter home.

The wind shifted as Carolyn changed direction to clear the point toward Villasimius marina. The sail billowed with a quick snap followed by a long dreadful tearing sound.

"Ugh! A rip in the mainsail," she shouted. "Just what I need!"

Before the cave incident she'd planned to hike with Griff to the promontory, rent a scooter, and photograph the flamingos. But even before the rip she'd lost all interest in sightseeing. Now, all she wanted to do was to get supplies, repair the sail, and get the hell away from Sardinia.

They motored to the east of the marina, opposite the bay's large arc, and anchored. They'd have to take the dink over to the island. Carolyn wanted no neighbors, as usual, but even more so tonight. Although quite a few yachts were anchored out, they were far enough away to suit her. She was exhausted and scared. The sail needed repaired, and she needed rest. Then she would figure out what to do next.

She cleared the headsail reefing line that led to the reefing drum at the bottom of the forestay. Satisfying herself that it should run free, she returned to the bow and untied the sheet lines that control the sail. She always kept them secured to the bow pulpit railings while in port.

Leading the port line aft, she took a couple of turns around the winch and cranked it to unwind the sail, then rolled it up by the roller furling rig. Roller furling, she'd learned from Augie, is how a sail is reduced or completely furled by rolling it up using a line, a drum, and swivels. By keeping its bow pointed into the wind while moored it was not a problem getting the sail rolled out. She untied the sail halyard from the cleat and began lowering the sail. After letting out a yard or so, Griff folded it flat along the side deck. She lowered it again while he folded. They repeated this until the whole sail was on deck.

While the sail took up little space rolled up on the forestay, it was a mass of stubborn canvas on the deck. Tugging and cursing they wrestled it into a clumsy bundle and tied it up with a mooring line. They sat at the dining table for a few minutes deciding to reward their strenuous effort with a nice dinner.

Griff hauled the bundle aft where he heaved it unceremoniously with a loud thud into the dinghy. The bundle filled the small boat with one edge hanging over almost into the water. He pushed and pulled on the mass until he made room enough to sit by the motor to steer. Carolyn sat on the sail lump, thinking company at the dock might not have been such a bad idea, after all.

After motoring into the marina, they tugged and jerked the sail into an uncooperative marina cart before weaving and rolling it to the sail repair shop. After examining the sail, Carolyn and the seamstress agreed on a price. Carolyn was surprised. The quote wasn't a huge gouge. She knew marinas overprice their services because sailors have few options.

She'd repaired the smaller sail herself when she first bought the yacht, but she was tired now and this was a job too big for her.

"For such a large marina, there's not a handicraft shop or boutique in sight," Carolyn said, surprised at the small village, considering the size of the marina. It was on the tip of Sardinia and ships passed through from all over the Mediterranean.

"You'd think they'd have more restaurants?" she said to Griff, dusting the dirt from her arms.

"This reward dinner won't come easy, will it?" Griff asked as he rubbed away the sweaty grime lines circling his neck with the bottom of his T-shirt. He pulled a ragged wallet from his cargo shorts and held it open in front of the scooter rental guy.

"Give me that," said Carolyn. She pulled out a few euros to pay for the scooter and returned the wallet to Griff.

They hopped onto the scooter and took off looking for a restaurant.

Griff's expression lightened, along with his red face, after resting in comfortable dark wicker chairs in the shade of lemon trees and white parasols. The pistachio green and cream painted stucco walls of the only restaurant they could find open leant a cool ambience to the warm afternoon.

"Hot as white lightnin' simmerin on a copper coil," Griff said, stroking back his hair.

"But it's a dry heat, darling, not like the South," Carolyn said as a joke.

"Dry heat, my ass! It's so damn Fahrenheity around here, it'd roast a lizard."

Despite the heat, Griff ordered meatballs and mozzarella, described on the menu as a classic Neapolitan dish with a twist. The twist was rice. Carolyn ordered giant gnocchi with cherry tomatoes, ricotta, and smoked cheese.

The waiter suggested sangria, the house specialty. He was back in no time with large icy goblets of red wine filled with fruit, laced with spice and brandy.

Carolyn downed hers and ordered a second glass. She felt relaxed as the sun heat her cheeks and the sangria heat her insides. As she looked at Griff and saw that concerned look was still there and she knew he was worried about her. Someone worrying about her wasn't familiar to her, and she wasn't sure what, if anything, to do about it.

She reached out to touch his hand.

If he stayed much longer, she'd need to explain a few things. But they hadn't made a commitment. He might be gone tomorrow, who knows?

Since they had to wait a few days for the sail repair, there was time to explore the area as she had originally planned.

When they got back Carolyn hopped on the deck as Griff steadied the dinghy and then handed her the bags of groceries they'd purchased from the marina. Carolyn took the bags to the galley to put things away.

As Griff reached his foot over the water to step onto the boat, the dinghy moved in the opposite direction. Trying to catch his balance he flailed his arms in the air and yelled.

Splash!

Griff walked in the galley soaking wet with an embarrassed look on his face. Carolyn looked at him in confusion for a second before she realized what happened.

"Darling! You've taken the plunge," she laughed.

Griff didn't think it was very funny, but was happy to see her laugh. He smiled.

Carolyn couldn't stop laughing. She sat down in one of the swivel chairs and held her stomach. Tears rolled down her face and she couldn't catch her breath. She knew it wasn't *that* funny but she couldn't help it.

All her pent up emotions let go. And it *was* a little funny after all. They were supposed to be pirates, cavalierly chasing about on the Mediterranean.

Griff slogged off to a hot shower. Carolyn eventually calmed down, but the much needed smile stayed on her face.

After he'd cleaned up in the shower and felt he'd regained his dignity somewhat, he stretched out on the lounge with his head propped up by a couple of large white pillows to relax after his harrowing dunk in the sea.

A thick apricot band of color stretched above the horizon like the thin residue of Armagnac left unforgivably in the bottom of a brandy snifter. Intoxicating stripes of golden yellow hovered above those smooth shades of peach. Shooters of ruby and violet swilled the heavens like a purple-rain cocktail, heavy on Curacao, and chased the close of another day. The magic hour.

The next morning Carolyn slid on a pair of shorts and a halter top and sauntered to the galley. After a quick cup of coffee, they motored into the marina and secured the yacht. She didn't want to take any chances trying to get the repaired sail onboard from the dinghy after what had happened yesterday.

She grabbed her Nikon DSLR and a thin orange kilim, threw them in her large straw bag, and flung it over her shoulder.

Griff rented a Vespa while she reported to the dock master. They'd decided to visit the flamingo lagoon after all, before picking up the sail. He barely slowed to pick her up in front of the harbor office before she'd grabbed her hat and hopped onto the back.

Carolyn clung to Griff's waist as they putted off toward the nesting area through mile after mile of large cactus clumps and scrub trees lining the sandy road. After finding they'd taken a wrong turn somewhere, they drove over a slight rise and the massive lagoon came into view.

"Wow! Have you ever seen anything so beautiful?" she asked.

A narrow strip of sandy beach separated the shallow lagoon from the sea. It was the perfect sanctuary for the vivid coral colored birds to breed and nest.

Like hundreds of children's party noise makers, all flats and sharps desperately out of tune; the off-key chorus ratcheted the noise louder as they approached.

They spread out a blanket on a lovely grassy spot overlooking the water. After shooting a few shots to use later for inspiration in his paintings, Griff stretched back to take a nap. He'd dozed off before she'd even reached the edge of the water.

The flamingos, not particularly shy, didn't mind her. One pair nuzzled and twisted their long necks together as if they were sharing secrets they didn't want to share. But in general, they squawked all of their other business. Occasionally a young one got curious and looked directly into the viewfinder, almost touching the lens. She hoped the automatic focus would work.

A few of the elegant birds began running in the shallow water. They spread their wings, craned their necks forward in unison, and took flight like a fleet of jet planes.

Carolyn would compose a picture, get ready to shoot, and they would turn away from her at the exact same moment.

"Damn! Twenty beautiful shots of the back of flamingo heads," she said.

Did she have the luck, or what? Well, of course she did, she thought, glancing at Griff on the blanket.

Tired and hot, she headed back to the blanket. Griff heard her coming and sat up.

I'm gettin' hangry," he said. "Cross between hungry and angry. Best be getting' me fed soon," he laughed.

It was dusk when they made it back to the marina, returned the scooter, and picked up the sail. They loaded it up by setting the setting the cart on its side and rolling it in and then rolled the cart back to the boat.

As they were wrestling it aboard, she laughed thinking of him falling in.

"Be careful, there," she said.

He nodded and gave her a look.

"I wouldn't be worth two dead flies if I let this fall in the drink? Is that what you're tryin' to say? I am already painfully aware darlin'. Painfully aware. I'm afraid if it happens again, I'd have just enough pride left to saddle up a June bug and skitter off."

"Skitter off to where?" she laughed again.

Griff only grinned.

They struggled getting the sail in position, but decided to wait for morning to put it up. They decided to stay at the marina tonight.

"I need to finalize the course to Sicily," she told him as she made him a cheese sandwich. Griff looked puzzled as he tore into the sandwich and shrugged his shoulders.

"I'm in," he said as he headed off to bed.

After checking the weather and plotting the course, Carolyn loaded the pictures from the day onto the computer. She scrolled through, hoping to find one or two amazing shots out of the hundred or so she'd taken.

She often told herself that all good photographers took a million shots until they got a good one. It wasn't just her, all the while shaking her head knowing it wasn't exactly true. Photography was an art. She had a little talent, but knew she wasn't as great as she would like to be. As she looked over the pictures a small spot caught her eye. There was someone in the pictures.

Was someone following them? Watching them? He was far off, but, what the Hell?

She took the clearest one, as all of them were not in perfect focus, and magnified it.

"Jeeze! It's that cop, Tomas, from Cala Ganone. What is he doing here in Villasimius? Yes, it's a smallish island, but getting from one place to the next was not like driving downtown in a major city. It's a journey."

And didn't cops have, she paused trying to think of the word, jurisdictions?

She went to the galley and pulled up the floor board under the sink. With her pistol in her pocket, she went up on deck and looked around, trying to appear nonchalant. The harbor was quiet with only a few people walking around near the marina store. She bent to look under the dining table on her way to check out the lounge.

She'd stowed her chain in the hidden compartment under the sink and retrieved her gun. Satisfied that no one was on board, she set the alarm, and went below. Fortunately it had cooled down, and she closed and locked the window before quietly crawling in next to Griff. She slipped the nine millimeter under her pillow and kept her fingers gripped around the handle.

Fear crept over her as she stared at the deep bruise circling her ankle. Her shoulders twitched and her eyelids fluttered as she forced herself to concentrate on the stars.

It was well after midnight when she dozed off.

The forecast was light with seas at less than a meter. But once they were out in the open water, the wind steadily increased to twenty knots with gusts of over thirty. The sea kept building and soon the waves were over six feet. It wasn't dangerous, but she wondered, *if the forecast was so wrong to start, was it going to get worse?*

After several hours, another boat, which had been lagging behind The Kiss Goodnight turned around and headed back to Sardinia. She thought about doing the same. It was a tough decision, but she realized that turning back meant beating it into a strong headwind and arriving in the marina after dark.

Not a good idea.

They kept going. Fortunately, the wind leveled out and didn't get much worse, but the seas kept building to over eight feet. This was the roughest sea she'd ever sailed.

The Kiss Goodnight handled the conditions with little fuss and held the course well. Occasionally a breaking wave hit her at the stern to push her off course and she had to give a quick correction at the helm to avoid broaching.

The wind slacked off at sunset and gave them the chance to take a break, make a peanut butter sandwich, and rest on the lounge for a few minutes. Griff fought with his hair, trying not to eat it along with his sandwich as it batted his face.

"I'm tired," Carolyn moaned, as she realized for the first time she was too exhausted to run her fingers through Griff's hair. Or even care if he had hair.

Soon after sunset, the wind strengthened again to twenty-plus knots. It howled through the riggings like a lost and lonely sea wolf as white caps broke all around them. Griff's steady, firm stance behind her kept her warm and less afraid. It was her biggest test in sailing so far, and she was very happy she wasn't alone.

She looked back at him; *I wonder if he's had enough of this little adventure yet? At any rate, he had no choice now.*

At about midnight they approached the halfway point between Sardinia and Sicily where the shipping traffic was the busiest. They took turns manually steering and dodging the yacht between commercial ships.

At 5:00 a.m. they reached the quiet wind zone off the coast of Sicily. The wind was completely dead, but the sea continued rolling.

"As idle as a painted ship upon a painted sea," Griff said. "That's from The Rime of the Ocean Mariner. See, I'm not such a landlubber after all."

"It's Ancient mariner," Carolyn laughed. "And yes, darling, you have gotten to be quite the mariner."

At daybreak, a pod of seven or eight dolphins greeted and swam alongside them. They were great company until Carolyn had to turn the engine on to get them back on course for San Vito.

After they passed through the doldrums - the no wind zone - the breeze came around again. Carolyn turned off the engine while Griff used the autopilot to put up the sails. They sailed three more hours until shrouded mountains of Sicily's northwest coast appeared through the mist.

She turned the motor on again and motored through the mirror flat sea in four knots of true wind until they reached the anchorage outside of the San Vito marina.

They dropped anchor. Both sorely needed rest after the arduous sailing.

Carolyn poured herself a stiff shot of bourbon, no tea. Griff just went below. When she finished locking everything and went to join him, he was fast asleep. She lay down to watch the morning sky and before she knew it, she was out.

Carolyn woke in the afternoon to the heavenly smell of bacon frying.

Before she could get out of bed, Griff came in with a small tray holding an espresso while promising a delicious breakfast. So she lounged in bed in her master cabin while he served breakfast. The room was rather large, the largest on the yacht, with mahogany walls, floors and teak beams on the ceiling. There were two large windows, one on either side of the queen-size bed. It was as comfortable as any bedroom she'd ever had.

She enjoyed feeling the soft sheets of brushed Turkish cotton and a thick white goose-feather filled down comforter folded up at the foot of the bed keeping her feet warm. She retrieved the luxurious cushy pillows that she'd tossed to the floor and propped several behind her back, sipped her coffee and enjoyed gradually waking up.

Not having a clue how Griff might react to the news of the policeman at Villasimius, she didn't know how to broach the subject. She didn't even know what she thought of it herself. It was all very strange.

It might be a good time to fill him in on her past. But it might have been a coincidence too, and now that they were in Sicily, it doesn't matter.

Carolyn's brow wrinkled in concern. She'd have to think it over. It'd been a long day and night of sailing and she needed more rest.

Every muscle in her body hurt as she reached for the pictures. She decided to look them over again before she mentioned anything.

After spending most of the day in bed, she walked out on deck. It was dusk, her favorite time of day. The mountain behind Cabo San Vito cast a long shadow over the low-lying flat plain and bay.

Wall to wall beach umbrellas of the holiday resort were set up in blocks of bright color. A sea of bronzed bodies in various stages of packing up their towels and bags were ending their day at the beach. Some stayed put, deciding to wait and watch another spectacular sunset before heading back to their hotels. All of this was mere background for the theatrical show of gestures as only Italians can do.

Griff was busy on Carolyn's computer so she grabbed a bottle of the wine she'd bought at Augie's vineyard, gave him a sloppy wet lick on the neck, and settled comfortably back in soft cushions on the lounge. She'd looked over the photos again and she was sure it was that cop, Tomas, at the flamingo lagoon. She still didn't know what to think.

The vivid light from the glowing amber sun lingered on the horizon, teetering, before it slowly surrendered. Carolyn held up her glass of wine, marveling that the color matched perfectly with the last gleam of twilight. Her nose hovered over the glass for a long moment, breathing in the rich red perfume as it let her mind conjure visions of aging wood, musty castles, and dark secrets that make your blood run hot.

Her thoughts flitted haphazardly like fireflies on a sultry summer evening. Glimmering with radiance for a moment before growing dim with only a chartreuse trail flashing through the darkness as a reminder. She tried to gather them, or at least focus on them one by one, but it was useless as they continued playing "hide and seek" through the night, paying no attention to her efforts to concentrate. A gray undercurrent of fear was at the center of each of those wayward thoughts that belied their luminosity. She nestled back to enjoy lingering on the sweet edge of overindulgence.

The first two glasses of wine went down easy. She was on her third or fourth glass and just beginning to relax when she turned the bottle over to pour another drink to find it was empty.

She stood up, stretched out her arms, moving her neck back and forth, and snapped a kink. Losing her balance, she plopped back down on the lounge. Griff's back was to her so he didn't see her stumble. She gathered herself together, pursed her lips in a fish kiss pout and tried to walk purposefully to the galley.

He mumbled "sure" when she asked him if he wanted a glass of wine. She came back with a bottle of Pinot and an extra glass for him. While pouring his wine, she glanced at the computer screen, wondering what was so fascinating. He closed whatever he was looking at and began scrolling through one of his social media pages.

"My adoring public is wondering what I'm doing," he joked.

She made a quick, albeit somewhat drunken, mental note of the suspicious behavior and headed back to the lounge to drink more wine.

She took another sip and propped the pillows around and under her so she could gaze straight up at the moon.

She remembered lying in the grass with her brother on magical summer evenings. But before long her mind wandered to Andrew. And then the cave. She realized she was afraid again. She was every bit as afraid as she had been as a child.

She poured herself another glass of wine.

CHAPTER 11

It was shortly before sunrise when Carolyn opened her eyes. A pinkish glow arching above Earth's curvature surrounded the yacht. The horizon separated the sky from the water by dark layers in shades of navy - the shadow of the Earth's edge. Soft red light scattered up through the pink twilight as the sun took an eternity to rise. It was the time of day, before dusk and dawn, when the light becomes enchanted. Of all the hours in her life, Carolyn loved the magic hours best.

Shimmering ripples, like jewels in a pirate's bounty, gently rocked the yacht to coax her awake. She'd drunk more wine than usual last night, but she felt good.

Nevertheless, she had a nagging feeling in the back of her mind. She shouldn't have allowed herself to think about Andrew last night. That was a mistake. She'd indulged in a private pity party. It always upset and distracted her. Thinking of him made her question herself. But this was a new day, and it was time to move on.

Griff was still sound asleep. When the coffee finished brewing, she poured herself a giant mugful.

She felt surprisingly well considering all the wine she had to drink. It was a good thing as she'd planned to sail to Vulcano that day.

Before her plans had been interrupted with the cave scare, Carolyn planned to visit Vulcano, the volcanic island off the coast of Sicily. She'd read about the mud spa and the hike to the crater to see the lava flow.

She drank down the first cup of coffee and was on a second when she heard Griff stirring in the bedroom. She brought him a cup and set it down next to him before giving him a firm kiss on the lips.

"Time to get up sleepy head."

As she pulled away, she ran her tongue across the whiskers around his mouth. He reached out after her as she walked away laughing.

"What's the hurry?" Griff groaned.

"The world beckons an exploration," she laughed.

She kept quiet about the possibility of a maniac hunting her being reason enough to keep moving.

Just as she lifted the anchor, Griff appeared on deck, sipping from his mug. With a thick head of hair still tousled, his disheveled appearance suggested he was the one that had over-served himself last night.

"Good morning, love!" she called to him.

"Where are we off to today?"

"We have reservations at a world class spa where we are going to pamper ourselves with the royal treatment," she said with a knowing laugh. She gave the wheel a turn and headed toward the island of Vulcano and the mud baths.

"Good, I'd like to get a haircut, too, while we're at it," he said.

Carolyn laughed again.

The Kiss Goodnight was magical as she danced between the sea and the sky all that day. With the wind as their mate, they surged through the buoyant waves spraying foam as her bow cut through the water. The bright blazing sun was a strong tonic, restoring her soul and replenishing her spirit. The whisper of the wind through the white sails and sheets rustled in perfect rhythm with the sea.

Off in the distance Carolyn spotted white trails of smoke drifting ominously ahead of them. It lingered like a long flat cloud above the black cone-shaped island rising up out of the Tyrrhenian Sea.

Griff lay reading on the lounge. Occasionally, he'd read an interesting observation aloud.

"The ancient Romans believed that the steaming tower on

the north shore of Vulcano was the workshop chimney of Vulcan, the fire god," he said.

"Look," Carolyn said as she pointed toward the black silhouette.

"Wow!" he said as he looked up.

"We got here faster than a knife fight in a phone booth," Griff said.

Carolyn laughed. "We've been sailing all day, darling. Well, I've been sailing all day."

"Your boat, your rules," he joked.

"My rules doesn't necessarily mean I do all the work," she teased.

"You *know* you'd rather do it yourself," he smiled. "And I need to edjamacate myself, anyway."

But with that, he put his book down and stood behind Carolyn as they sailed toward the eerie mountain.

They moored at Porto di Ponente on the western side of the peninsula, close to a smooth strip of black sand about ten minutes' walk to the mud pools.

Magnificent volcanic rock formations jutted out of the clear glassy water. The eerie protrusions cast long shadows on the curved stretch of black sand beach, one of the few sandy beaches in all of the Aeolians.

The whole scene was stunningly beautiful in an old monster movie sort of way. It wouldn't be too surprising if at any moment, Godzilla or King Kong appeared growling and gnashing its teeth from behind the Volcano. The rotten-egg sulfur stench that drifted through the air only added to the monstery sense of the place.

After dropping anchor, they lay on the lounge facing the volcano. She wrapped her leg over his as he held his arm behind her back and snuggled under the blanket. They entertained each other with scary stories while watching the sun hiss into the ocean. A hint of red glimmered from within the volcano, creating a dusky rose sky above the purple twilight.

The next morning, they docked the dinghy at the small marina and caught a shuttle to the resort. She'd made reservations to stay a day or two, because in reading the reviews of the mud baths, it usually took several days to remove the sulfur smell. A few days in the swimming pool and some spa pampering sounded like a good idea. She just wished it smelled a little more like Corsica.

Ah, Corsica. The memory of sweet smelling maquis drifted through her mind.

An elegant arched entrance and circular limestone drive welcomed them to the hillside resort. The carved out black mountain embraced the enormous white stone building and lush green grounds. North African architecture in the lobby, influenced by the Moroccan tradition, featured stunning lancet arches and walls of tadelakt lime from the Marrakech plateau. Craftsmen used river stones to rub undulating surfaces into the smooth lime walls. Accentuating the walls were huge frames of beautiful Zellige mosaics, pieced together like a puzzle from small, differing-shaped, hand-painted ceramics.

The earthy shades of the tile, bold yellows, rusty reds, deep purples, and natural browns had naturally muted over time. In contrast, an amazing range of intense cool colors accentuated the soft subtle shades. A decorative sign in beautiful Islamic script announced, "A Tribute to the Land and Sky from Casablanca to Marrakesh." A small plaque underneath read, "An art that has been passed on by master craftsmen, the process not changing in a millennium."

She touched the tile, noticing how perfectly flat it was, while waiting for the bellboy to help take their bags to the room.

Their room was large and comfortable, but its most noteworthy feature was the view. It was on a high floor that looked directly out to another island, not far away.

After dropping their bags in the room, and changing into their swimsuits, they headed to the pool for a swim before dinner.

The veranda and pool area was every bit as lovely as the lobby. Mostly blue mosaics, darker than the water, accented the top edge of the pool. They ordered a drink at the bar. Even though alcohol wasn't customarily served in Morocco, this was Italy, after all.

They stepped over to the pool, holding hands, and jumped in together. After swimming and splashing for a few minutes, Carolyn swam to the edge and looked out at the young volcanic island close by. In a million years she could never have imagined herself here. Until her brother died, she'd have thought it crazy. She was in the middle of the Mediterranean on a smelly island with a man she adored.

They chose to dine at the pool to enjoy the panoramic view instead of going to the room to change for the dining room. The garcon wheeled out a tray with two large salads to start the meal. It was the most unusual salad either of them had ever seen. Bulgur, dates, pistachios, oranges, and spinach were mixed and served in a big, round, shallow clay bowl. A macerated orange and shredded cilantro flavored the oil-and-vinegar-based dressing. It was hearty with sweet and sour notes. Griff didn't like it, but Carolyn thought she would need to try it a few more times to develop a taste for it.

Next they wheeled out a large brown clay pot that sat flat and circular with a large cone-shaped cover. The waiter called this a tagine and explained that the cover design is to promote the return of condensation back to the bottom of the pot.

The common method of cooking in the North African desert where there is a shortage of water is slowly, over coals. The waiter further explained in broken English, that tagine is a savory stew made with meat, chicken, or fish with vegetables. The common spices used are ginger, cumin, and turmeric. The word tagine is also the name of the distinctive pot they use to cook the stew.

Next to the tagine was a large basket of flat bread or as the garcon called it, khobz. They played it safe and ordered the chicken.

"Deelish!" Griff said as he pushed back from the table. After dinner, they walked over to the railing and watched the last of the light fade from the sky. Griff wrapped his arms around her and nestled his chin in her neck.

"Tomorrow is our spa treatment, you know. We have to hike over there," Carolyn said as she pointed toward the brown area just beyond the marina dock.

"I thought this was the spa, Kitten?" he asked with a confused look.

"I love when you call me kitten, but no, my darling. We passed the spa on the way here. It's the mud baths," she said with a giggle.

"Well, gosh dang it," he said with an exaggerated drawl. "That there looks like a pile of horse squeeze."

She could tell he was kidding, but still obviously disappointed.

Carolyn couldn't help but laugh.

"Wear something you want to throw away when we're finished, like maybe that batman T-shirt you bought in Corsica," she said.

"I will have you know that T-shirt is a collector's item, my dear, ripped neck and all."

He pursed his lips with faked anger. Carolyn reached up and kissed him with her own pursed lips. She held his face in her hand for a moment and smiled at him.

The next morning she wore a bikini she'd purchased in Paris under her oldest sundress. She didn't have an old bathing suit, like the travel guide suggested.

Her diamond and gold anklet stayed hidden in the boat with her gun. She definitely didn't want to take the chance of losing her most precious gift in the mud. The guidebook warned there might be a chemical reaction with sulfur mud and gold. She knew what that meant. If it *may* have, it *would* have. Griff put on his oldest pair of swim trunks and they headed off to the mud pools. Or the horse squeeze pits as Griff called them.

Away from the resort, closer to the pits, the odor became more obvious. Apparently the way the resort cut into the cliff caused the noxious fumes to blow by without lingering in the nose as much.

They brought along some towels that the hotel kept for guests visiting the pools. Even those had the rotten egg smell, albeit with a delicate flowery note of laundry soap trying to disguise it. They paid the few euros to get by the gate and paid a few more for the shower afterward. It wasn't much of a shower, though, and most people just went to the beach and washed off in the ocean for a while before rinsing the salt water off in the shower afterwards.

Stepping into the warm wet mud felt like stepping into the chocolate pudding. Of course, she'd only dipped a finger or two in the pudding. And the mud smelled more like boiled eggs than creamy chocolate.

Carefully walking through the warm mud, she spotted an area about the size and shape of a large hot tub. She slogged her way to the tub noticing that some areas were hotter than others were. Thermals running from the volcano heated the mud.

Easing down into the gritty dark mud she closed her eyes,

THE KISS GOODNIGHT

enjoying the warm, relaxing ooze on her legs and hips and then tummy and breasts. As she slouched back against the rock wall, she dipped down until her chin was covered. She tried not breath in too deep.

"Oh, it's heavenly," she told Griff. "Come on in, the mud's fine." She laughed.

Griff walked toward her, rocking in a back and forth motion like a gecko parsing out its steps. After each step, he stopped and looked around as if deciding whether to proceed. At any moment she expected him to dart back to terra firma.

"I'm perspiring, Carolyn. Is this considered exercise?" he asked in the lazy drawl he used for emphasis.

"In South Carolina we aim to stay out of the pluff mud. Folks would think I got ate up with the dumb ass if I tried to charge 'em to sit in this. And on top of that, now I'm hungry for shrimp."

"Whoa. You're hungry?" She laughed.

He eventually sat down and reluctantly agreed that it was quite wonderful once you got over the ick factor.

She stretched out her legs and flexed one foot then the other.

Pulling the thicker mud from the bottom of her "tub" she smeared it around her neck and all over her face leaving two holes for her eyes and one for her mouth. She even put a little dab on her eyelids. She heard the mud tightened up your skin, and she didn't want to be a total hard body with drooping lids.

After the thin coating of mud on her lids dried, she added another coat. They leaned back against the rock sides and closed their eyes.

They took turns mentioning the therapeutic benefits of their soaking, trying to convince each other that it really wasn't a crazy thing to do. She began to notice that the warm water had a therapeutic effect on her bladder.

"I have to use the ladies' room," she groaned to Griff.

He just laughed. "I'll be waiting, right here in the mud. I can't see how a little pee would make a difference here, darlin', but you go on ahead,"

She walked to the boardwalk and headed over to the primitive bathroom. When she turned the corner, she jolted to a stop. Tomas stood about ten feet away from the ladies' room.

What the hell? she thought.

After a moment, she realized he didn't recognize her and continued into the ladies room.

She tried to think. Why in God's name would he follow her?

Surely he was following her. You don't just run into people on these islands. He must work for Andrew. He's not a cop. Cops don't travel from island to island.

She was afraid to go back out and had to steady her nerves by realizing he wouldn't be able to recognize her disguised in mud.

After double-checking that she was still covered, she peeked out. She didn't see him.

She tried to walk casually without looking around and drawing any attention to herself. Her heart thumped a frightful tempo as the ringing in her ears grew from a whir to a low roar. She felt if people were to look, they could see the caking mud crack as it moved up and down over her beating heart, but she knew that was crazy.

She walked along the boardwalk platform, looking toward where she'd been sitting. Griff wasn't there. Glancing around the area, she saw him standing by the ticket shack. He was talking to Tomas. Both were looking around suspiciously.

She'd been walking behind a family of six. If anyone were looking, it might have appeared that she was part of the family. When they stepped into the pools she stepped in with them. She watched Griff nod his head with Tomas a few times then walk back to the "tub" spot they'd shared.

She sat there for a few minutes, contemplating what it might mean. Dumbfounded, she walked back toward the bathroom, just out of his sight, then turned around and came back.

"You've been gone a long time. Everything OK, sweetness?" he asked.

"Um … my stomach is a little upset. It must be the odor," she replied.

"I know what you mean," he said with a halfhearted laugh. "This whole island smells like the poop chute of a coon dog after a dead skunk festival."

"Ha ha." Carolyn feigned a laugh.

More like the stink of salty betrayal.

She sat down and looked straight into his eyes. He leaned his head back and said nothing more. She waited. Nothing. Not a thing. After a few minutes she said, "I think I've had enough. Let's go dip in the ocean."

She got up, and he followed her to the ocean. The water was clear, the same color as pictures she'd seen of the Bahamas. She dived in, rinsing the dried mud off with her hands. She dove down, picked a pumice rock from the bottom, and used it to scrub her legs and arms. It made the mud come off easier and it was a natural exfoliate.

Her brain kicked into high gear. She felt disconnected from her surroundings and her situation. It was as if she were a hawk, circling overhead watching this insidious scenario. The burn from scrubbing her leg too hard brought her back.

She dove repeatedly, rubbing her face as she swam under the water, perhaps subconsciously trying to wash away what she'd seen.

She didn't want to confront Griff about seeing him talk to Tomas. She wanted him to tell her on his own what was going on. He wasn't doing that. She was upset and confused, so she did what she always did, until she had time to think about things. Nothing.

Later that night, she lay staring out the window of their hotel room, thinking, while Griff lay asleep beside her.

She groaned as he tried to pull her next to him.

"The mud pool was too much for me. I just need to sleep," she said as she closed her eyes and waited to hear his soft snoring.

Billowy clouds hung in front of the moon as it etched the rugged black shapes from the neighboring island on a canvas of shimmery silver water. As she lay gazing into the dark beauty, her eyes opened wide. She remembered Griff closing the page on his computer when she walked by to give him a glass of wine. He'd switched it to his social media page.

She thought about that for a while.

He has obviously been in touch with Tomas. But why? Was Andrew the only one she should fear?

The thought that Griff might work for Andrew slowly made its way into her consciousness.

She wondered how she could've been so stupid. How could he know Andrew? He couldn't have possibly known that she would invite him to her boat, her bed, and into her heart.

She became acutely aware of his foot resting on her leg while he slept, so she gently moved from under it. The thought of him touching her caused her to hunch her shoulders.

Not consciously deciding to leave, she found herself quietly getting up and grabbing her bag. Griff shifted in the bed and mumbled.

"I'm not feeling well," she said as she headed in to the bathroom. "I'll be back in a minute."

She dressed quietly and opened the door, listening for his soft snoring.

Yes, he's fallen back to sleep.

She opened the door to the hall, slipped out, and closed it. It didn't make a sound. She slung her bag over her shoulder and made it down the hall to the elevator without making much more sound than the deafening friction of her pant legs rubbing together. When the door opened with a loud ping, she looked around, stepped in, and pushed the button to the lobby in one swift motion. It took forever for the door to close, even with pushing the button continuously. The night clerk looked up in surprise when the elevator door opened and she stepped out.

"I have an emergency at the marina," she said. "I have to get out there right away."

"There is no one to take you at this hour, madam," he replied with a firm but with concerned tone.

"It's an EMERGENCY!" she said with her bottom lip quivering. "It's only a five-minute drive. Couldn't you take me, please? No one will be up for hours."

He shook his head no, then looked around for a moment and grabbed the keys to the shuttle van and said, "Come on. Let's go."

He tried to keep up with her as she walked out to the van and just barely got the door clicked unlocked when she yanked it open and threw her bag on the floor of the front seat. She glanced back to see if anyone had awakened to the sound of their shoes crunching on the volcanic gravel. The entire time she whispered to him how much it meant to her that he was taking her and how kind he was.

She kept talking, thinking that if she stopped, it might give him a chance to ask her about the real reason she was leaving in the middle of the night. And she wasn't exactly sure of the answer. She just knew that her boat was her safe place, and she needed to be there *Right Now*.

When he pulled up to the dock, she handed him a wad of money that equaled about twenty dollars, but he refused to take it.

"No, madam. I help the beautiful woman in distress. It is reward enough."

"Thank you so much," she said and tossed the money on the seat while struggling to get the bag.

A moment later she was pulling the engine cord, and miracle of miracles, it started first try. She was surprised. It never started on the first try, but adrenaline pumped through her like a cigarette boat running from the DEA when she'd yanked on that thing as if her life depended on it. The sudden roar of the dinghy coming to life shattered the soft gray silence of the night.

The back of the boat dipped down, and the nose flew up as she turned the rudder toward her yacht and zipped out into the harbor.

The words "A clean get-away" ran through her mind. She drove out to the yacht at full tilt. After pulling up next to The Kiss Goodnight, she hopped aboard, turned on the operating lights, and cranked up the dink.

A noise coming from inside the galley caused her to slow down the pulley so she could listen. A shadow stood in the doorway.

Without hesitation she dove under the lounge and pulled out the spear gun while at the same instant her mind processed that the hulking mass on her boat was BUG. She'd named him BUG in her mind whenever her thoughts drifted back to Maine and the "Big Ugly Guy."

He was next to her in a flash and knocked her down on the lounge. She fired the spear gun and hit him in the right bicep. The way his head lurched forward on his neck confused her.

She'd seen this man before. Before Maine.

"You fucking bitch!" he screamed in a voice surprisingly high pitched for a man of his size.

With one swift jerk, he pulled the gun away from her and tossed it over the side splashing it in the water. He swung his arm around, backhanding her across the face and knocking her back onto the lounge. She scrambled up on her knees grabbing the railing to jump over the back of the boat. Bug grabbed her by the collar of her shirt, lifting her off the mattress. Her legs flailed out, landing a good kick on his thigh. It was as solid as a tree trunk.

A piercing crack followed by a quick "psew" of rushing air came from the island.

A bullet found its mark in Bug's chest with a soft "dooosh" sound just before he groaned and staggered to the railing. He stumbled, trying to grasp the rail as he fell overboard.

In the stillness following the splash, Carolyn heard the shot reverberate on the volcano and echo four times. She jumped to the floor and crawled over to the yacht lights. Her hand shook so hard she had to steady it with her other hand to flip the switch.

Hunkered down, she listened into the night. Hushed waves lapped against the boat while the only thing she could see were a few harbor lights and the stars.

She scooted, duck-walk style, to the anchor, and again used both hands to flip the switch. While the anchor came up, she crouched to the engine and started it. She pulled the yacht's wheel halfway around once, steering toward the open sea. When she was far enough off shore, out of rifle range, she stood up.

The hair around her scalp pulled tight and her teeth clenched on themselves as she realized that the man who'd just been shot and fallen overboard, was the maintenance man at her brother's funeral.

Grabbing the throw from the lounge, she wrapped it around her shoulders, cocked her chin upward, and headed into the darkness.

CHAPTER 12

Carolyn motored another hour, until the lights from land were barely a twinkle, and dropped the anchor.

She gasped as she entered the galley. Everything was a mess. Same in the master bedroom. Everything was tossed and torn.

Bug was looking for something. But what?

She went to the galley and checked the floorboard under the sink.

"Yes," she sighed, at the sight of her gun and anklet.

She pulled her hair back in a ponytail and put on a pot of coffee.

"What's he looking for?" she asked.

She stood in a daze watching the coffee drip in the pot. The steamy rich aroma revived her as she poured herself a cup. She took a sip as she hunched her shoulders in a hopeless shrug and headed up on deck.

Gonna be a hot one, she thought as she sat sipping and trying to think.

Three cups of coffee later, and no closer to figuring it out, she decided to clean. She started in the salon and ransacked in the opposite direction. Everything Bug had pulled out and looked through, she looked through and put back.

At three o'clock in the afternoon, near exhaustion, she stopped for a couple of cookies and some cold coffee. She'd finished going through everything and straightening up in the master bedroom, so she lay down on the bed eating and looking at the ceiling. Still not able to grasp why this happened, she went to the kitchen to get another cookie.

With one leg dangled over the arm of the chair, she swiveled around absentmindedly nibbling on the cookie.

She knew the who, when, and where, but what about the why? She tried to focus as the crumbs fell into her shirt.

"Ah! Nothing," she groaned as she stood. "Time for a glass of wine."

The low-pitched glug of the cork easing out of the bottle popped in Carolyn's mind. As the soft hiss of sweet aroma escaped to fill the air with fruity oak, random thoughts formed in her mind.

Wine, computer, Griff hiding his screen.

She clicked on the computer and sat impatiently, waiting for it to come fire up.

"Come on already," she said as she rolled her hand in a circle in front of it, encouraging it to boot up faster.

She hated all the weird terms for everything computer related. When she'd gotten her first computer, she'd wondered why she needed a mouse.

A mouse? She hadn't needed any pets. She smiled remembering it.

She jiggled the mouse and began scrolling through the history. Griff hadn't been very good at covering his tracks as the first thing that popped on the screen was the name and contact information of Tomas. Tears brimmed her eyes making it hard to read, but there it was. An email from Tomas.

So, he had contacted that cop, or whatever he was.

In that moment of loss, an aching gut-wrenching emptiness washed over her. She hadn't been aware of the depth of feeling she'd for Griff until it was gone. The pain of loss ripped over her like quick gust of ice-cold winter wind.

Tears streamed down her face as she began to comprehend she'd suffered another betrayal. Another piece of her heart withered to scar tissue on her already-battered soul. Her choking sobs felt hollow in her chest.

"I think I might have loved Gri… him," she said bitterly, not able to say his name.

THE KISS GOODNIGHT

"God, I am so stupid!" she cried. "Soooo stupid!"

After a while, her tears exhausted themselves and her brother's voice came in her mind. "Sis, you're the strong one between the two of us," he would say. "You only need to see it. It's in your heart."

Carolyn rarely cried in those days. The days before Mike died. She'd had little need of poetic quotes about crying and feelings. It all seemed like such a luxury then. An indulgence for people with nothing better to do than worry about how they felt. She'd never had time for that silly luxury.

But since his death, she had plenty of time for tears and sorrow and all kinds of grief. She knew he had been sincere about her being strong, but it gave her a terrible feeling.

"If I'm the strong one, we're in big trouble," she would say to him. They would both laugh.

She took a couple of deep breaths, closed the computer, and went to get herself a glass of water.

She'd stored a box of Stephen King books she'd found in a vintage bookstore in Paris. After rousting through them, she found one she liked and began reading it again. Stretched out on the lounge under the canopy she let the gentle roll of the yacht soothe her, as she got lost in the story.

It was the only way to quiet the thoughts in her mind.

She would read several pages, realize she had been thinking about Griff, Andrew, or Tomas, and have to go back and reread the pages. She struggled to get her mind back to the book as she'd hoped that eventually her subconscious would come up with an explanation. She found this way of thinking best suited her, putting questions on the back burner and letting the answers boil up to her conscious mind.

After the fifth day, she decided if she stayed much longer, she needed to go fishing. Most of her fishing experience was by spear in the shallows.

The sails were down and secured and the rudder tied over hard to the left. She threw a float from the bow and the stern and put the ladder down. She didn't want her boat sailing away from her while she was fishing. It was a long swim to shore.

She put on her snorkel gear and bent under the lounge for her spear gun.

"Oh geeze," she said. "How could I have forgotten that?"

Bug had thrown it overboard right before he tumbled over after it. She tried not to think about the shot that sent Bug overboard, or who might have shot it, as she went to look for a rod.

She pulled a rod off the rod holder Augie had installed in the smallest berth he'd transformed into a closet/storage room.

Augie insisted she take the tackle box and rods with the boat. After she'd learned how to spearfish, though, she'd had no interest in rod fishing. It was so boring. She was thankful the old guy had been looking out for her. She grabbed the seven-foot rod with a fast action and 20lb. fused line. She hadn't paid too much attention to him while he explained the fishing gear, but seemed to recall a conversation about better casting with this line. She opened the box and found a few lures in a plastic bag.

Once she opened the bag, she realized why they were sealed. They looked and smelled like shrimp. Old, long dead, shrimp. She took the box and rod out on deck. After the sulfur smell at Vulcano, which had taken three days to wear off her skin, she wanted no more noxious odors lingering on the boat if she could help it.

She fumbled around with the hook and the smelly rubber bait, trying to secure it. She didn't want it nibbled off.

Now wishing she'd paid closer attention to Augie, she vowed to go sailing again as soon as she got back. She'd have him teach her how to fish. Augie would love that.

After three tries at casting, she just let the fishing line hang in the water off the side of the boat.

Oh well, it was a hook in the water. Either a fish would swim up and bite it or not. She wondered what difference, if any, casting skill made.

"I guess Augie will tell me."

She picked up her book and began where she'd left off - halfway through the story of Misery. After a few minutes, she set the book on her lap and fantasized about hobbling Andrew, and maybe even Griff, as she closed her eyes and dozed off.

The persistent jerking on the line woke her, and she hopped up to crank in a two-kilo Sea Bass.

THE KISS GOODNIGHT

"Mmm," she said. "Thank you, fish. Thank you, sea," she said, trying to be mindful of the sea god Poseidon and the lessons Augie had taught her.

Carolyn gazed across the wind-ruffed surface. The sun shone off the rippling water to radiate the changing hues. She closed her eyes and drew a breath of balmy fragrant air.

Peace, she thought.

For over two weeks The Kiss Goodnight undulated in quiet contentment. The hours became days, rolling by in undulating rhythm, like the transient scatter of the white tipped swells that stretched across the blue expanse in every direction to the horizon… ever changing, yet ever the same.

The pounding fear and anguished confusion that scratched with long tenacious fingers in the dead of night grew softer with every dawn. Suspended, drifting, somewhere between the calm sea and the chaos of her mind, Carolyn's nerves began to settle.

The weather had been sublime. Gentle breezes whispered warm assurances as it kissed her sunburnt cheeks and tousled through her hair, now auburn from the sun.

For the thousandth time, she tried to piece together what had happened. Other than Andrew being a vindictive, narcissistic psychopath, she had no explanation for his behavior.

And that freaking cop, or whatever he was, why had he followed her?

No matter how she wracked her brain, she found no explanation for that either. Most importantly though, why would Griff secretly meet with him.

No matter what the reason, he betrayed her.

Although her tortured heart glowed red in anger at Griff, she ached for him. Despair and loneliness had threatened to devour her whole those first few nights, but she'd refused to allow it. Just before her tears threatened to consume her, she'd breathe deeply, fill the holes in her heart with icy coolness and her vulnerability would once again be chilled behind the façade of coping. Just as she'd fought the fear of those phantom monsters in the attic those long years ago, she fought this. She knew no other way.

Her eyes glistened as she pulled out the ship's log.

She studied the charts, maps, and weather, and plotted her course. Second-guessing herself with every choice, she eventually chose the course least likely to put her in the path of anyone she knew. Or used to know.

Andrew sent Bug looking for something that obviously wasn't there, and if it had been here, it was down in Davey Jones's locker now. Along with him.

She was sure she wouldn't be seeing Bug again, or anytime soon, at least. The idea of being fish food next to Bug at the bottom of the sea caused her to shudder.

She eventually concluded that Bug wasn't looking for anything; Andrew only sent him to harass her. He was such an ass. A dangerous vindictive ass.

She gathered her heart and mind and decided it was time to move on. The cookies and wine were long gone at this point, and she felt she was losing her civility. That thought made her think of an English tea with a delicate lemon tart topped with plump juicy raspberries and a sugary cinnamon crusted scone dipped in clotted cream waiting to be washed back with Earl Grey tea.

"Washed back?" she laughed as she pulled up the anchor. And so with the fear of becoming so uncivilized as to wash back Earl Grey Tea, she set sail.

The most predictable course would be through the Straits of Messina, between Italy's boot and the island of Sicily. It was the fastest way to the Eastern Mediterranean, but the traffic was heavy through the narrow strait and she thought it best not to take the chance of being found. She was sure they would look for her there. She would do better out on the open sea.

Cool gusts of air blowing about four knots whipped over the waves in a low whistle as she sailed back toward the tip of Sicily.

She held her chin high as she passed San Vito Lo Capo, refusing to remember the feelings she shared there with Griff.

After a quick stop in Marsala on the western coast to pick up supplies and fuel, she set sail, or rather motored off with a small amount of apprehension about the weather. She thought about stopping at Porto Empedocles to visit the Greek ruins in the Valley of the Temples, but with the next weather depression headed her way, she felt she was still too close.

Too close to what? To Andrew? she thought.

She decided to go straight on to Malta. She felt an aggravation growing in the back of her mind beyond her normal fear and hatred toward Andrew. The decision to skip the Greek ruins had made it clear.

She was running.

CHAPTER 13

A dull mist wafted silently as it crept over the surface of the calm sea. Carolyn had enjoyed the morning, and with little effort, caught another 1.5-kilo sea bass. Although tired of fish, she remembered the two previous weeks when the food situation had been grim.

By evening, the wind had strengthened and shifted to the west, allowing her to sail at a healthy seven knots.

A whiff of burnt sulfur lingered in her nose a mere second before shooting her with alarm. She glanced over the yacht in a panic and then turned to scan the horizon.

Thick, growing plumes of ash, like hellish genies escaping a giant black bottle, spiraled in the sky several miles behind her.

The radio crackled as she fidgeted with the channels until a clear transmission came to life.

"An earthquake near Mt. Etna, measuring 3.2 on the Richter scale, has collapsed a side wall of the volcano!" the radio announcer blared.

Carolyn fumbled with the binoculars to get a bead on the corkscrew of smoke as it billowed higher and higher. Ash particles danced through the hazy air, sparkling and glaring like dragon eyes, before the sun dimmed behind the ghostly beastlike puff. She stood transfixed at the sight as a quiet worry began to take hold. Things might get rough.

She headed for the galley to prepare peanut butter sandwiches in case she'd be stuck at the helm. There'd be no time to sit for the tea and crumpets she'd purchased at the marina store if things get dicey.

Well, tea and cookies, anyway.

As she donned her inflatable life vest, she had the bright idea of attaching a water bottle to its side, just in case.

It was a brilliant idea and she thought herself very clever.

But later, as she rested near the helm, she wasn't quite as impressed with herself. Every time she leaned back, the lump either dug in the middle of her back or pinched under her arm.

The beginning of the depression arrived in the early evening with a series of small showers and squalls. Intermingled with muddy ash, the driving rain belted the horizon from low slung clouds. Beads of grotty rain trickled over Carolyn's exposed skin as each passing feeder band intensified the ache in her bones. She squinted into the gray layers.

Things looked like they might get dicey.

But other than rain in her face and achy bones, she thought she was managing well.

As the mistral wind turned to blow from the northwest, the sea rose from the stern. The swells grew to eleven feet and the long rollers separating them came faster.

She'd already furled the sails and continued sailing downwind under bare poles, with no sail at all. Augie swore by this tactic, calling it 'running off,' but it required steady hand-eye coordination, he'd warned. She'd need to keep the back of boat perpendicular to oncoming waves. If not, a wave could push her around and catch her broadside. She wished again that she'd spent more time with Augie, sailing, and paying closer attention. Her concern was mounting even though the yacht was taking the waves well.

At first, Carolyn actually enjoyed riding the waves. The feeling of weightlessness as the waves push you across, up and down, gaining speed. You're floating on nature, gliding effortlessly, one with the sea, on top of the world.

Even though most sailors considered it a last resort, she was beginning to think it was easier to sail with the waves behind, pushing, instead of straight on.

But after a quick shift of the mistral, the yacht turned, and she found her stomach churning as furiously as the roiling sea.

Carolyn held her breath as the bow of The Kiss Goodnight crested a mountainous slope of water and then surged down into the trough. Sea spray and rain bombarded the deck as the drum of wind filled the air with a primeval electric charge.

She braced herself against the helm as a mammoth wave reached over the deck and bashed her in the face. A fraction of a second after the deafening thunderclap inside her skull, a loud ringing, as loud as the impact, began blasting in her ears.

As her head inflated with pain and noise, Carolyn lost her sense of balance and her legs buckled. She gripped the helm and held steady. Drenched and shivering, fear throbbed through her pulsing veins.

These were the rogue waves from the earthquake, she realized as she tried to convince herself she would be OK. They were sure to dissipate soon.

Her arms trembled and grew weak as she struggled to keep the nose of The Kiss Goodnight pushing forward into the storm. The wind had begun with a rushed whisper as it tore across the ocean's surface. But as it gathered pressure, it became a whistling moan, screeching through the increasingly violent surges.

She was fine, she reassured herself. Only the wind had her spooked.

"Hey, Boreus. God of the devouring winds. I thought we had a deal? I gave you the very best sparkling wine!" she shouted.

As the wind and sea continued to twist and gyrate in horrifying unison, an unnerving scream was born. The haunting sound was nothing one could imagine, unless of course your childhood nightmares were of Raw Head and Bloody Bones. Once you've heard it, you realize there's no mystery why stories of the sea were so full of hideous monsters and grotesque mythical sea serpents.

Carolyn half-expected a colossal Kraken to reach up from the sea bottom with a tangle of beastly suckered arms, clicking jaws, and gnashing sailor-bone teeth to confirm with the glare of its giant eyeball to be the source of the unholy scream.

The wind gusts continued to increase, and the waves lashed around the yacht as if the sea were erupting in a demonic boil. Carolyn furiously blinked her salt encrusted eyelashes as her hair flailed, whipping her face. The yacht was going faster than she could handle, even with no sail.

She gripped the helm with both hands and leaned back to steady her footing as the boat nosed straight down another large wave. The bow plunged, burying itself into the back side of the rising wave ahead, almost causing the boat to pitch-pole end over end.

"Where the hell did that come from?" she screamed.

As the boat rocked and lurched before the next plummet, she ran to the stern and threw off two sea anchors, one on each side. Biting rain stung her face and hands as she hauled out all the heavy rode and tossed that in, as well. When the boat headed down into the next wave's trough, her vantage point allowed her to see the giant wave building behind her. It looked higher than the mast but she guessed it to be about twenty-five to thirty feet. A groan escaped her throat and her heart dropped with the realization that *these* were the rogue waves from the radio warning.

She gripped the helm with her arms grasped up between the spokes and pressed her entire body hard against it. Even with the parachute anchors deployed and using all her might, she didn't have the strength to hold the yacht straight.

She was no match for the sea and her arms and legs grew weary from the pounding swells. She held firm but muscle fatigue and chill caused her to shake.

"I'm losing control." She moaned.

One slight release of the helm as her bicep quivered and the yacht spun . An enormous wave caught the bow broadside and the raging sea washed over, under, and around her. As she flew through the air, she remembered…

"Harness!" she screamed.

She took a deep breath before being catapulted down, deep into the ocean. The god-awful banshee screams stopped as she shot down. For a moment, the only sound was water rushing past her ears. The forceful hurtle toward the center of the Earth slowed and then stopped.

Silence.

Oblivion.

Complete darkness.

Carolyn floated in nothingness for a moment before the vest began to pull her in the opposite direction. After what seemed an eternity, she broke through to the surface. The waves chopped and pummeled her from all sides as she gasped for air. She glimpsed the yacht as she struggled in the surf but realized she couldn't get close enough in the crashing waves even if she were able to swim. The yacht would smash her.

Another enormous wave struck and pushed her under with it. She choked and snorted salt water when she surfaced again while trying to wipe her eyes of the burning froth.

She was able to catch only half a breath before the next roiler came. At the last moment she attempted to dive through it, but was too late and it crashed her into a head over heels tumble. When she regained herself, she tried to find the yacht again. It looked close to one hundred yards away. She could see that one of the masts was gone.

I'm going to drown.

It was the first time the thought entered her mind.

After another crashing wave finished shaking her arms and legs like a tiny rag doll, she caught her breath and looked for the boat again. It was gone. There was nothing now. Nothing but her. And the ocean. And that horrible screaming wind.

She forced herself into a zone, a tactic she'd been doing all her life. She closed her mind to all worry about herself and the yacht. She needed stay calm and feel the ocean. She needed to relax enough to breathe after each swell.

When a wave came, she dove under it and let it tumble over her. After about thirty minutes and nearing exhaustion, she saw the mast rolling about fifty feet away. She tried to swim forward, alternating between deep breaths and a wave-tumble routine. She was barely able spit out mouthfuls of salt water before the next wave hit.

Minutes passed like decades until she reached the mast. She calmed herself as the front end of the pole dipped down in the wave and came close. The mahogany pole began to roll away, but one quick grab and it was hers.

Thankful for all the snorkeling and fishing she'd done with the spear gun, she was familiar with swimming in waves. But even in her wildest dreams, swimming in this nightmare would never have occurred to her.

She scooted to the thicker part of the mast and wrapped her arms and legs around it.

"Aghh." she groaned in relief.

Her mind filled with all sorts of random thoughts as she tried to see the turbid horizon. But after a cursory search for the yacht, she found holding her head up took too much energy, so she leaned down, straddled the pole and held tight.

Before long, a chill overtook her. She feared the uncontrollable shudder might shake herself off the mast. She gripped it, closed her eyes and willed her mind to the sweltering tropics of New Orleans.

She imagined a sweltering August heat with angry yellow sunrays flaming over her unguarded shoulders as they bit and blistered her back. A heat so blazing that even on a summer afternoon under the shade of a lazy Spanish moss-covered live oak, you could fry an egg on the sidewalk if you had a mind to. Right there on the sidewalk. Even in the shade. She could almost hear the sizzle.

After a while, her consciousness of chill ebbed, and she was calm. She felt in rhythm with the waves and was thankful that she'd been successful at hanging on.

It was night when she opened her eyes again and became aware of the change on the sea's surface. As far as she could see, only bubbles and streaks of broken crests, backlit by moonlight, jounced up into foamy white caps. Gone was the pelagic maelstrom... the oceanic terror... gone... back to the fiendish hell from whence it came.

A tingle starting in her hands spread to her feet. She was afraid to let go and stretch for fear of a wave knocking her off, so she wiggled her fingers in an attempt to increase the circulation. As she grew more confident, she extended her stiff, numb appendages further and further, one at a time, until she felt a soreness in her thigh. After situating herself to get a better look, she noticed a deep gash extending down her leg between her hip and knee. A small trickle of blood still oozing from the gaping wound dribbled into the sea water.

Carolyn hoped what she'd read about sharks smelling blood

from miles away was an exaggeration.

"Not too many shark attacks in the Med," she remembered Augie saying. She clung to those words.

At midday she awoke and slowly unclenched her stiff arms from the mast. The sea was calm once again. It took some time, but she was eventually able to sit up and straddle the mast to look around.

Her life jacket was hot and uncomfortable but she reminded herself how thankful she was for it. As the feeling in her arms and legs returned, she tried sitting this way and that, on the mast in an effort to find a comfortable position.

The heavy feeling on her thigh surged in a burst of pain. A wave of searing fire seized the quivering wound, intensifying the brutal agony with each movement until the wave faded and dragged off, drawing her mind into sweet oblivion with it.

Carolyn grimaced as she maneuvered the water bottle and took a sip. She dipped her hair in the ocean and draped it over her face to keep from burning and then clenched the mast again and closed her eyes to await another wave of pain.

The soft coolness of the dusk breeze blew over her skin to awaken her again. When she positioned herself astride the mast, she was startled to look up and see a boat.

Tears welled in her eyes and her gasping sob spilled them down her sunburnt cheeks.

She hunkered down on the mast and began to paddle. After her thought about drowning, she hadn't allowed herself to think anything about this situation. Nothing.

An hour later, she watched as the sun dipped below the sea just behind the boat. As the fiery ball etched its silhouette, Carolyn found hope in its shadow, that it might be The Kiss Goodnight.

She kept paddling, sometimes vigorously, or as vigorously as she could, and sometimes just barely. She tried to ration her small bottle of water, now thinking that she'd been a fool not to attach a two-liter container to the vest.

When dawn broke the following day, Carolyn found she'd paddled to within two hundred yards of the boat. She wept as she instantly recognized the beautiful and glorious fine lines of The Kiss Goodnight. Not lost to Poseidon's treasure chest after all, she rocked and rolled in the gentle wind, patiently waiting for her mistress's return.

A slow smile spread over Carolyn's parched, gaunt face until her bottom lip cracked and the hint of copper tasted on her, dry, swollen tongue. Relief warmed her, as the burning sun never had.

Carolyn tilted her face toward the radiating shafts of light. It was as if the treacherous waters of the savage ocean had permeated her with an overwhelming sense of thankfulness. She allowed herself a few tears of joy before attacking her course with renewed vigor.

After reaching the yacht, Carolyn floated as she stared up at the six rung climb. The tight skin on her sunburnt arm pulled as she stretched it toward the ladder. Her stiff fingers curled around the dangling rescue bar of the bottom rung. She gripped the, thin, cold, metal, slumped her shoulders, and exhaled a deep sigh.

With one hand clinging to the step, Carolyn lurched toward the yacht with her other hand extended high over her head to reach the next bar. As she left the mast, it dipped below the surface and then rolled away.

She wondered how she would climb up as she leaned her head back to gauge the effort it might take. Her leg, excruciating now, was useless. She reached for the next rung, and getting what little grip she could, began pushing and pulling to force herself up.

Carolyn celebrated each success with light-headedness and the worry that she now had further to fall back into the sea. There were no safety harnesses here, and she was sure she was too weak to save herself if she fell back in. Her muscles burned and her hands grew tired of holding on.

She had two choices. Her exhausted fingers or a long way down.

After climbing each rung, she entwined her arms between the bars so she couldn't fall until the sensation of spinning and blurred vision eased. She wasn't sure, but she might have passed out twice before the waves of pain in her thigh subsided. After it numbed, she dragged it up with her as dead weight.

CHAPTER 14

Exhausted, Carolyn pulled herself to the top rung. She braced her body against the hull and nudged her trembling foot up to the toe rail. After hauling herself up waist high, with every bit of remaining strength she had left, she swung herself over it. She teetered on top of the rail before heaving forward to land on the deck with a thud.

Her fingers opened and closed, stroking the smooth teak floor as great heaving sobs racked her body. Her thick lashes, clumped shut with thin crusts of salt, blinked grateful tears from her swollen bloodshot eyes. As the tears subsided, she wiped her forehead and brushed the sticking strands of hair from her face. She sat up and a weak smile cracked open her chapped lips.

"I made it!" she cried hoarsely.

A long hour later, she crawled into the galley and drank everything she had in the fridge.

She hobbled by hanging to the walls and crashed into the bed.

Two days later, giant, angry lizard eyes beaded down on her as a blowing flame shot over the cracked eggs she imagined on her forehead.

With a stiff, store hand she blinked and rubbed her eyes. Her body ached and her forehead glistened. A sickly chill ran down her spine and her cheeks burned with flush when she saw her thigh.

I'm in trouble. She groaned. *Real trouble.*

She limped to the kitchen. Her puffed and swollen lips cracked and bled as she drank down a warm soda.

After gathering a knife, towels, water, and vodka, she hobbled to her bathroom for a sewing kit, cotton swabs, and the leftover antibiotics she hadn't finished.

Pain shot through her knee and she winced with each step as she carried the supplies to the lounge area. She set everything on the table and examined her leg. There was a long gash between her hip and knee. The skin around the deepest part of the gaping cut was dark, almost black. Red lightning bolt lines shot from its center. It was so sore and swollen that it hurt to even touch it.

After pouring herself a glass of vodka, she tossed back a swallow. Grimacing and coughing, she did it again. She waited for it to kick in while she prepared the needle. As a girl she remembered seeing her little grandmother, a half-blood Cherokee, sew together a deep cut on her knuckle with a needle and thread. It'd been horrifying to watch. Now she would find out how horrifying it was to do.

Carolyn lit the candle she'd purchased to create a romantic ambiance for Griff. It caused her just the tiniest bit of heartache before the feeling passed. She held the needle and knife over the flame until the steel blade turned blue and then scorched black.

She set the knife on the table and took another gulp of vodka before splashing the knife and the wound. After a deep breath, she cut into it. Tears filled her eyes and her teeth clenched tight. She blinked feverishly in an effort to squeeze away the tears so she could see. After another deep gasp, she cut deeper until she reached the source of the infection.

She grunted as she dug into it and then rinsed it with water until it looked clear. A gut-wrenching moan stifled in her throat as she poured vodka over it. She raised her eyes to the sky and waited for the burn to subside.

Still whimpering and breathing heavily, she doused it again. With the first stitch, the white thread became pink with blood.

"Oh God!" she cried. "This wouldn't hurt this much if the leg wasn't so swollen and sore. She pulled the thread as tight as she could and pinched the skin together as she tried to close the gash. The skin around the wound had formed tough edges from the seawater. Every few stitches she'd splashed it with more vodka and then rested her head on the table to catch her breath. Thirty stitches later, she doused the whole thing.

After swallowing a double dose of antibiotics, she remembered she hadn't eaten in days. She would vomit them for sure on an empty stomach. Not the least bit hungry; she dragged herself to the galley and opened a pack of oatmeal cookies.

"Thank-you," she mouthed to the sky as she munched a cookie. She was glad she'd loaded up with supplies at the Marsala marina. Especially the vodka.

After a long rest in the swivel chair, she grabbed her book and supplies and dragged herself back to the lounge. She looked out across the water with amazement.

It was hard to believe the sea was so calm. She'd need to find to a safe harbor as soon as possible.

Even as she thought those words, she knew she wouldn't be going anywhere in the near future.

That night the fever broke. She awoke feeling much better despite being stiff and sore. Feeling like a human for the first time since the giant wave washed her overboard; she took a deep breath, poured herself a cocktail of warm ginger ale and vodka, and washed down another double dose of antibiotics.

***

More than a week passed as she rested and healed from the storm. The cookies were soggy, but she'd happily eaten half the pack. Standing was still a struggle, so she took her time and stretched back and forth, checking her condition, and making sure she was steady. Other than the sore leg, she was in fair shape.

"The Mediterranean Mast-rider-Gash-sider diet," she laughed. "I wonder if it will become the new craze."

Somewhat surprised that she found that funny, she realized that she felt lucky to even be alive.

She'd been going light on vodka now, not wanting to contribute to her dehydration any more than was necessary, but felt she still needed at least a small amount of anesthetic.

As she watched the sun's golden rays dim in brilliance as they welcomed the encroaching night, she felt the breeze of mercy flow over her like a soft cool sheet.

Several times now, life has taken me to the brink, only to

bring me back again.

She'd survived she realized with a powerful surge of pride.

The more she realized what she'd just survived, the angrier she became.

Who was Andrew to intimidate her? She'd never run or hide from him again. She'd face that bastard.

That's it!" she said. "I'm finished!"

With a slight grunt and a drawn out groan, she held her stitches together and hobbled to the anchor switch. She slapped the toggle, yanked the rope to start the chain, and swung the wheel toward Malta.

CHAPTER 15

It was late afternoon when she motored into Manoel Island Yacht Marina on the island of Malta. The crew on the dock stood waiting to help as they'd no doubt seen the broken mast. They tossed her two bow lines, but when they saw she was limping, one of the shore men jumped aboard and helped her tie up to the electric and water. She thanked them and then went back in to lie down.

As it was sundown, she decided to stay on the boat and check in with the dock master in the morning. This was the only place on the island where she could get a new mast and she wanted to have the dinghy engine looked at, too. Amazingly, it hadn't washed away, but she was sure the engine had been drenched and needed checked out. But that could wait until tomorrow. She went below after a quick lock up and laid down. It had been quite a while since she could simply relax.

In the middle of the sea, you are on constant vigilance, always looking and watching, worrying about hitting things or things hitting you. Watch duty in the open sea is usually divided between three sailors. By herself, she'd made due. Even though her watch duties had sorely lacked the last week, she'd managed with no further problems after the storm.

So, she felt relieved. Now that she had a power connection from the dock, she popped some popcorn. After adding a dash of the blended seasoning Augie had given her and a heavy sprinkle of Parmesan cheese, she opened her last bottle of red wine and turned on the TV. With a bit of effort she parked herself in the middle of the fluffy bed.

She sprawled out over the bed appreciating the advantage of being alone.

A short story on the news about three tourists from England drowning in the storm caused Carolyn to shudder. She'd been alone for almost three weeks now, not seeing or hearing any news.

She thought about Griff for the first time since the storm. She wondered where he was.

Maybe he'd continued his tour of European art galleries, or he might have even gone home to see if he could work things out with his ex-wife. Or he could still be with that Tomas character plotting subterfuge against some other woman. That was silly, she knew. She felt sad that things hadn't worked out with Griff. But remembering him talking to Tomas without saying a word to her about it struck a flash of anger in her expression. She fell asleep listening to a true crime show about a woman poisoning her cheating husband. She smiled as she drifted off, humored by her taste in lullabies.

***

She glided on thermals, dipping and diving, and then soaring again, high above the cliffs of Sardinia. The faint air of pine forest mixed with the fragrance of the sea was the essence of her waves. Not a care in the world on her mind, she felt the strength of the wind lift her wings higher and higher. As she circled around in the warm updraft, an object caught her eye. A lovely yacht tied next to the sheer limestone cliff beneath her nest. She glided toward it to investigate. She dipped lower and lower. The object was her yacht. As she flew closer, she noticed two people sitting together at the table. A panic came over her. As she flew even closer, she saw the dark-haired man grasp the woman's hand. His face was full of compassion. As she flew around to see the woman's face, a shriek tore through her beak. The woman was her.

***

Carolyn startled awake. It took a moment to realize she was in her bed. It took a few moments more to realize she was in Malta, not Sardinia.

She went to the galley for a glass of water and turn off the crime channel, wondering why she had such vivid nightmares. She returned to bed and slept soundly the rest of the night.

Her first thought upon waking was of Tomas. He was the man in the dream. She was in the dream too as a screech owl and as herself. She thought about his hand touching hers. Had that happened? She tried to remember. She'd been so upset about the cave incident that she hadn't noticed at the time.

Maybe he had touched her hand with concern. What of it? He was doing his job, consoling the nearly murdered victim at his seaside town.

Of course, she'd told him she might have imagined someone grabbed her ankle and she'd probably just slipped. She knew he hadn't bought it. But that look he'd given her. What was that?

It wasn't the look of someone skeptical. It was the look of concern. Deep concern. It looked like genuine caring.

After thinking it over, she concluded it was only a dream.

She opened her computer and waited for it to fire up while she headed to the galley to make coffee. Her leg looked god-awful with its Frankenstein sutures, but it was feeling much better. That reminded her to make sure she got more antibiotics today. She would need to see a doctor. She went back to the computer sipping the steaming coffee as she sat down. Having had no coffee for more than a week, she'd missed it.

With her nose inside the cup, she breathed in the aroma as she hit the history control on the computer. There it was again. Tomas's email.

She began her e-mail:
Why the hell have you been following me?
No, that wasn't right.
She remembered the look on Tomas's face in her dream.
"What was that?" she asked herself again. Then she wrote:

Dear Officer,
I have no idea what your problem is. I told you I'd been mistaken in the cave. You do not need to follow me. I will pursue some sort of action if I need to. Please leave me alone.
Carolyn Wingate

As she showered and dressed, she heard the ping of a reply on the computer.

Dear Miss Wingate,
Thanks God you are OK. I must talk with you as soon as possible.
Tomas

"Thanks god you are OK?" she said to herself.
"Yeah, I thought that, too, Thanks God I'm OK."
She continued getting dressed.
After stopping at the dock master's office and arranging a ship carpenter to come by in the afternoon to give her an estimate on a new mast, she hailed a cab to the business district. The cab driver dropped her off at a doctor's office that was familiar to him. He'd taken more than one person from the marina to see him, he'd said.
After waiting only a few minutes, the doctor slowly slumped into the room. His one good eye focused on her in a curious way. The other eye squinted closed. He reeked of cigar smoke and she got the distinct impression he'd just set down a huge stogie before shuffling in to see her.
His bushy eyebrows reaching up toward his tousled gray hair and his lips turning down in an exaggerated frown made her second-guess her decision to seek medical attention.
After looking at her leg he opened his one good eye wide and then tilted his head instructing the nurse to bring a few shots of an anesthetic. Then he went to work. He nodded his head constantly as he reassured her that it looked worse than it was. Of course she knew that wasn't true, but she appreciated his positive attitude. When his hand deftly worked to reopen the wound, Carolyn laid her head back and closed her eyes. He cleaned it then re-stitched it, muttering in a smooth comforting voice the entire time about how fine it would be.

After he finished, she asked him if she could sit in the waiting room and rest for a bit. The wound was painfully sore again and the cutting and probing had taken a lot out of her. After twenty minutes, the anesthetic wore off and her leg began to throb. Before the pain got too intense, she headed to a pharmacy next door to fill the prescription for pain meds and a strong antibiotic.

The girl behind the counter at the pharmacy called a cab for Carolyn and *'Thanks God'*, Carolyn thought, it rolled up right when the prescriptions were finished. She hobbled out, got in the cab and after giving the cabby the address; she leaned her head back on the car seat and closed her eyes. The pain came over her in waves, like it had during the storm, but she dared not take the pain meds until she got back to the yacht.

By the time she got to the dock and paid the cabby she was in tears. The walk from the marina to her slip was one of the longest walks she'd remembered ever taking.

Apparently the doctor, despite his appearance, knew what he was doing. She'd peeked at him working on her sore leg with his scalpel as if he were selling Ginsu knives on QVC TV. She shuddered at the thought.

Her leg felt like a raging mass of gnarled flesh as she dragged it up to the slip. She stopped, took a deep breath, and steadied herself for the step onboard. She really didn't want to fall in the water now. Just as she stepped over, Tomas rushed up and held her elbow.

"Damn it!" she said. "You almost made me fall in."

"Carolyn, Thanks God you are OK," he repeated the words from his note. "I have been worried of your life."

"Who are you and what are you doing here?" she shouted.

Tomas brought out a badge and Carolyn glanced at it, in too much pain to care.

"Fine! Fine!" she said.

She hobbled to the sink and downed two of the heavy-duty pain-killers.

"I can't talk now, really," she said. "Give me a minute."

Five hours later she woke up and saw him sitting in the salon in one of the swivel chairs, swiveling slowly back and forth watching the television. She took two more pain pills with another gulp of water and slept until the next morning.

THE KISS GOODNIGHT

The sound of the marina carpenter calling from the dock cut through her foggy grog. She opened her eyes and dragged herself out on deck as fast as she could manage. After negotiating a price for a new mast in her broken Italian, the carpenter said it would take a minimum of two weeks to repair it. She hobbled back to the galley to make coffee.

A note on the counter read:

Carolyn, I went to shore this morning for a few things. I will be back shortly. I must speak with you. It is very urgent. Tomas.

"He has nothing to say that I want to hear. Either he is working for Andrew or he's another crackpot just like him. He can't possibly be a policeman. No cop has the time to chase some random person around the Mediterranean!" she said.

She rustled a few items into her bag as the realization that packing a bag and running from some jerk was becoming all too familiar. She felt an equally familiar rage growing as well.

How'd he get that police boat in Cala Ganone? she wondered, as she stepped to the galley.

She reached in her hidden compartment under the sink and removed her anklet and gun. She slipped the gold chain with the broken clasp into her bra but decided to leave the gun where it was.

Even though her leg still hurt like hell, and she was stiff from lying in bed most of the day before, she found herself zooming. She stopped at the marina office, paid a month's dockage in advance, and finalized the repair of the mast with the harbormaster. She stepped out of the office, checked for Tomas, and then waved over a cab.

"I need to get to the airport, please," she said.

The handsome, young driver gave her the once over, and then replied OK with a wolfish grin as he hopped out to open the door for her.

These young European men are so handsome, she thought absently as her nose wrinkled with the whiff of an unpleasant odor.

After heading out of the marina, the driver turned north. Carolyn knew the airport in Malta was toward the southern end of the island.

"Airport please?" she reminded him.

The driver nodded and spoke in a cheerful voice that she didn't understand. He glanced at her through the rearview mirror and flashed his reassuring smile.

They rode along a few more minutes before Carolyn realized he still wasn't taking her to the airport. She reached over from the back seat and said "airplane" while making a flying motion with her hand. He nodded his head up and down. His slick combed-back hair shining from the sunlight streaming in through the half opened dusty window revealed itself as the source of the stale, olive oil aroma.

"Yes, yes." His broad smile revealed several chipped and missing teeth.

Carolyn sat back and watched out the window for a few more minutes. Whey came to the end of the island and rounded the hairpin turn that headed back the other way she realized then that he was taking the long way.

She leaned over, her face within an inch of the driver's ear. The smell of rancid olive oil permeated the entire front seat. The driver kept facing ahead but rolled his wide eyes sideways toward her. The dark mole under his eyelid twitched up and down.

In a voice a few octaves lower than her normal voice, Carolyn slowly and clearly, so as not to be misunderstood said, "Do *not* fuck with me, buddy, I've got nothing to lose and I do *not* give a damn!"

After a brief silence, Carolyn leaned back in the seat. Neither of them spoke another word.

When the cab pulled up to the airport drop-off lane a short time later, Carolyn grabbed her bag, stepped out, and walked straight into the airport. The cab driver said nothing when she didn't stop to pay.

His smile was gone.

CHAPTER 16

After buying a ticket and getting her boarding pass to the first flight out of Malta, Carolyn stood last in line at the gate, still seething. She'd arrived later than planned, thanks to the taxi driver.

What if she'd missed the flight and had to wait all day for the next one? she thought as she muttered, "Asshole!"

She'd stepped into the passageway for boarding when she heard someone shouting her name.

"Carolyn, Carolyn!"

Tomas and Griff were stopped at the security gate. Her eyes bugged out as her head pulled back in surprise. The stewardess, unaware of her private drama, motioned her to hurry along and although her legs felt like overdone spaghetti, she wobbled through the gate. Her inner switch turned to autopilot in an attempt to prevent herself from reacting to the piteous look on Griff's face.

She heard the commotion at the gate get louder as she walked down the ramp to board the plane.

Not until the plane door closed shut, did she heave a sigh of relief. Neither Griff nor Tomas were getting on this plane now.

In a small part of her brain that wasn't as easily shut off as she'd hoped, wondered what Griff was doing here. She wondered what Tomas was doing here, as well, although she'd gotten familiar with him following her around.

She wondered why the hell they cared as feelings of self-doubt tried to pierce her resolve. The thought occurred to her that she might not be doing the right thing.

The feeling loomed over her for a few minutes before she convinced herself that Griff had had every chance to tell her what was going on back on Vulcano.

He hadn't. His mistake. She realized she had good reasons for her lack of trust. And she'd learned one thing for certain. Now that her brother was gone, she could only rely on herself!

Carolyn situated her throbbing leg and swallowed half of a pain pill. She'd just laid her head against the window and closed her eyes when the static voice of the stewardess came over the speaker.

"Seats up, tray tables back. We will be arriving in Istanbul in twenty minutes."

Somewhere deep in Carolyn's soul she knew that she would eventually make it to Istanbul, the city where her brother's life had ended. The city where her own life had ended - the only life she'd known, anyway. She contemplated the idea that this might have been her intended destination all along.

The flight path took the plane over the whole of Istanbul. For a city often covered in haze, clouds, and smog, the clear blue sky allowed her an amazing aerial view.

Carolyn pivoted in the tiny seat and leaned to see out the window. Large tankers and cargo ships lined up on the shores of the Asian side of Istanbul waited their turn to make the journey along the Bosphorus Strait toward the Black Sea.

The Bosphorus Bridge, six lanes of concrete and steel spanning the Bosphorus Strait carried a streaming assortment of vehicles across the gateway between the land masses of Europe and Asia. From the sky, the traffic appeared to be flowing smoothly, like an army of jungle ants swarming cooperatively with one another. Carolyn occasionally referred to the map in the magazine as she followed the Bosphorus Strait back toward the Sea of Marmara.

The estuary, known as the Golden Horn, joined the Bosphorus Strait at the Sea of Marmara to form the narrow peninsula known as Old Istanbul. On the tip of Old Istanbul she located the Topkapi Palace gardens and the domes and spires of Hagia Sophia and the Blue Mosque.

"The Golden Horn geographically separates the historic center of Istanbul from the rest of the city, and forms a sheltered harbor that has protected sailing ships for thousands of years," the magazine read.

Maybe I'll be safe here, she grimly thought to herself.

She put the complimentary magazine in her bag and gazed down over the dusty, terra cotta city with an absent-minded interest.

A thought gripped her heart.

The exact spot where Mike died is somewhere down there!

Pain rose from her heart to glisten her eyes as she wondered when the mere thought of her brother wouldn't cause her to feel gutted.

Carolyn found a room in a small boutique hotel in an old stone building on the Asian side of Turkey. This was as good a place as any to rest and heal her leg while she waited for the mast on The Kiss Goodnight to be repaired. The studio room, sparsely appointed, had actually been a veranda, converted into an enclosed room. A row of window panes attached to the main building angled out to the edge of the balcony, like one side of a pyramid, making it all glass from the ceiling to just about a foot from the floor. A population of colorful ring-necked parakeets that had adapted to life in Istanbul, where the winters are fair, lived in the eaves right above her window. She chirped along with them and even kicked out a painful dance step or two in rhythm to their melodic tweets.

She placed the chair where she could sit and look at the stately Bosphorus Bridge. Beyond the bridge, the view looked over the water, past the old city walls built in the third century and onto the many Mosque spires and impressive palace towers built on the seven hills of Old Istanbul.

While setting her few things in order, she limped from the dresser, to the bed, to the window, as if pacing out her daily routine, and then she sat in the chair and surveyed her castle, such as it was. It certainly wasn't her grand yacht, but it would have to do for now. She'd taken the first thing she could find. She needed rest. It occurred to her again that she was tired of running.

***

After two days of listening to Turkish pop on the small radio and falling in and out of sleep, Carolyn awoke rested at a little past one in the afternoon. She spent the rest of the afternoon flipping through the free magazines from the plane.

At dawn the next day, the call to prayer blaring from the tapering minarets of the surrounding mosques prompting the faithful to their prayers, called Carolyn to breakfast. It reminded her of the tornado drill sirens that wailed in her Midwest town on Wednesdays at noon, only these were much louder. The call to prayer has a much more pleasing sound than a siren too, although it took a while to get used to hearing it five times a day.

She stood at the window and watched as the bright orange glow of sunrise bathed the bridge and the six spires and dome of the Blue Mosque in morning light.

Her brother had loved this place, and she was beginning to see why, even though she resented it for taking his life. She limped to the hotel's waterfront café and took a seat closest to the water. A wrought iron railing, curving out over the strait, lined the paved patio. A worn rope dangled over the rail leading to a colorful boat bobbing up and down in the water. It didn't appear tied, just loosely thrown over, like a casually tossed lead on a well-trained horse.

Looking out over the bustling waterway of the Bosphorus Strait, Carolyn sat watching the sun glint on the bridge as she sipped a bitter sludge of Turkish coffee. Adding six sugar cubes into the delicate cup made it palatable. The waitress asked her if she wanted breakfast. She hadn't named anything in particular and hadn't offered her a menu. So Carolyn simply said yes. It felt like days since she'd eaten.

A short time later, the tray arrived filled with fresh sliced cucumbers, tomatoes, and plump, ripe, oil-drenched olives. A giant bread roll with feta cheese baked into the center, a glass jar of honey, and a tiny ornate spoon graced the tray. The savory cheese bread roll dipped in the sweet honey was heavenly. Another dish to add to her top ten list, now overwhelmed with nearly a hundred! The waitress stopped by her table and asked if she would like a Nescafe as well. Apparently Nescafe was the generic word the Turkish used for regular America-style coffee.

"Oh yes, thank you," Carolyn said, relieved. It would take a while until she would ever crave Turkish coffee. She sat sipping the

Nescafe and watching the harbor until the sun was well up in the sky. She felt much better today. Her leg was still sore, but the improvement was amazing. It had been a long time since she'd felt this well.

After a long nap, she woke to the thought of Andrew's face while grabbing that stabilizing bar and reaching for that oar buzzed in her brain with the same irritation as that boat engine had. But she felt good now. She would ponder those irritating thoughts later, she thought as she walked along the street to see what the different cafés had to offer for lunch.

Street vendors selling giant round sesame seed encrusted pretzel-like bread from their carts and an ice cream vendor selling dondurma, the 'elastic' ice cream, entertained her as she followed her nose around the corner to an outdoor café. Colorful orange-and-white striped umbrellas lined the cobblestone walkway where tables-for-two lined the building.

After seating herself, the waitress promptly took her order. She'd decided on cigara borek, a rolled pastry stuffed with feta cheese that when fried crisp resembled a cigar. She also ordered a bowl of yellow lentil soup. With a squeeze of lemon, the soup became another dish added to her top ten list. She was going to have to expand that list to an encyclopedia if she traveled much more.

On her walk back toward her hotel she stopped to order a scoop of pistachio-flavored 'elastic' dondurma. A small crowd gathered to watch the performance. The ice cream man, dressed in a colorful red embroidered vest with a matching fez hat and a towel draped around his neck, pull the entire contents of the pistachio ice cream from a large metal bucket.

He twisted and twirled it on two long paddles, then clanged his bell shouting, "Guzel dondurma, Guzel Bayan," (beautiful ice cream, beautiful lady). He filled the cone and then extended it out to her, dangling it on a forked stick. As she reached for it, he flipped it upside down and pulled it away from her. The crowd laughed. He dazzled them with a few more entertaining moves before letting her take the cone. Thicker and chewier than regular ice cream, Carolyn found she needed to bite it, not so much as lick it as she walked back to the shore-side hotel.

She took a seat at the same café where she'd had breakfast

and ordered tea. A boy of about eight years old approached Carolyn dangling a heavy solid, hand-carved, copper tray. He held the large ring of the traditional hanging service tray with both hands and balanced it expertly while he scurried toward her. Not a drop of the black Turkish tea, or Cay as they call it in Turkey, spilled from the small, gold-rimmed tulip-shaped glass cups. A golden rim also adorned the porcelain saucer. Next to the scalding glass lay a ruby bejeweled spoon and an ornate brass bowl that held sugar cubes under an engraved metal dome. Carolyn plopped one cube into the steaming tea and watched it dissolve.

Her mind wandered to Andrew again, and to the evening they'd gone on the dinner crawl in New Orleans. She remembered how he'd lit the sugar cube on fire and drank the flaming cocktail. She'd been so impressed with him then. Everyone had been.

What could have gone so wrong? she wondered. She picked up a sugar cube out of the bowl and heaved it into the sea water wishing it were that easy to get him out of my mind.

The little boy, whom she hadn't noticed behind the planter waiting to serve her more tea, made a weird face, and then shrugged his shoulders.

He was probably thinking I was a crazy American, she thought.

And he'd be right, she thought with a smile.

CHAPTER 17

After the fourth day of taking it easy, Carolyn woke just before dawn to the Salat, the call to prayer. She wound the bandage from her leg and inspected her wound. She was very pleased with the way it was healing and decided to celebrate with shopping and sightseeing.

The aroma of apple tea lingered in the air as she finished her Turkish breakfast and then walked to the main thoroughfare to catch a taxi. After a moment of bickering about the price, she was traveling the short distance to the bustling ferry dock. She tipped the driver well despite bargaining because she knew it was a hard life and she wanted to be generous. She'd felt the need to haggle about the price, however, because she didn't like being treated like the tourist that she was. She knew it made no sense.

The dock was crowded with ferries, fishing boats, private launches, and container ships vying for space where the three bodies of water converged. A diverse crowd of last-minute passengers, wearing everything from Ipods and ball caps to prayer beads and head coverings, scurried aboard the ferry alongside Carolyn.

Overheard smatterings of conversation containing dialects from everywhere in the world entertained her while she jostled to find a seat.

The ferry belched a huge cloud of gray smoke into the already gray sky and indicated they were leaving shore by bellowing a long, deep-based blare from its foghorn. Seagulls circled overhead screeching raucously to the passengers below as they begged for crumbs of simit, the large rings of bread covered in sesame seeds resembling pretzels that many of the commuters were eating for breakfast. Several kindly passengers tossed a few scraps high in the air only causing the birds to dive bomb the boat and scream louder.

Carolyn took a seat on the bench lining the outside of the ferry and sat eating the melting chocolate bar she'd purchased at the concession stand. She looked around wondering where all the life vests were stored for this many people, and if they were easy to access. A few life preserver rings hung around the outside railing, but there didn't appear to be nearly enough.

The familiar feeling of being watched passed over her. It was that same sensation of dread she'd known so often before. She tried to glance around the boat, not drawing attention to herself, but saw no one suspicious.

Flocks of seagulls continued to screech over the diesel sound of the ferry as they passed the white marble Dolmabahçe Palace with its decadent façade and Chantilly-lace fencing. She heard one of the passengers explain to his wife that it was second only in beauty and extravagance to Versailles in France.

Carolyn snapped photographs of the picturesque skyline that crowned the seven hills of the Old City with an interesting collection of monuments and religious buildings.

The churches of the Byzantines and the Imperial Mosques under the Ottomans with their delicate minarets, distinctive domes, and massive buildings provided a photographer's paradise. And, in case she did have a follower, the stately mansions, summer residences of the Ottoman nobility, and the majestic stone fortresses that graced a million post cards doubled as a good reason to shoot the photos.

She might have become a tad overly suspicious, she thought. But whatever, she'd search through the photos later to see if anyone is following her.

Once they reached shore, Carolyn crossed the big square from the ferry dock to the entrance of the spice bazaar. The cavernous arcade with high ceilinged walls lined with shops selling spices, sweets, and nuts. In its heyday, the bazaar was the last stop for the camel caravans that travelled the four thousand mile Silk Road from China and India to the Mediterranean Sea.

The smell of roasting peppers wafting through the air caused

THE KISS GOODNIGHT

her to stop for a moment to watch a dapper young man grill fish. His homemade grill consisted of an old metal barrel with metal bars crossing the top. Whole fish roasted beside long green, yellow, and red peppers. Several large trays served as a makeshift table where he prepared his fish sandwiches to sell. The fish seller held a long heavy-crusted bread roll on the grill for a nice char before dressing the sandwich with tomato, onion, parsley, and lemon, and then sprinkling the whole thing with a generous handful of red pepper flakes.

Carolyn watched a stooped-over man, carrying children's bicycles and plastic kitchen ware all tied together in a stack reaching about six feet high, order a fish sandwich and then make his way to the mosque steps. He swiftly unloaded his pack, stretched his back, sat down next to the pigeon covered stairs to take a big bite of his sandwich.

As she watched this unusual scene, a boy of about eight and his younger brother approached her to ask if she would like to buy a packet of gum. She looked into their pleasant, beseeching little faces and gave them each a dollar. They looked at each other with big eyes, threw their heads back in a glorious laugh. Thrilled at their good fortune they continued to giggle and push each other as they ran away down the street. They were so excited they forgot to give her the gum.

Before entering the bazaar, however, she felt a tug on her dress.

"Bayan, bayan," the little boy said. "Your gum." He reached up his plump, sweaty hand and gave her the small packet of gum, grimy and worn from holding it in his hand for who knows how long.

"Thank you," Carolyn called after the boy as he ran back through the crowd. She tucked the warm gum into her purse.

An unbelievable meld of vividly scented, fresh, whole, and ground spices greeted her as she passed through the large brick arched entrance of the Ottoman era marketplace. Tables were piled high with well-organized bins of spice in every color of the rainbow, all carefully sculpted into pyramid shapes. Sitting below them sat sacks of loose-leaf tea that included everything from the black tea grown on the Black Sea coast to Rose hips to the very popular apple tea.

Hanging above the tables and bins were ropes of dried

peppers, hollowed-out dried eggplants, garlic bulbs, and weird yellow and brown pods unknown to Carolyn.

Displayed alongside the spices sat barrels topped with trays of jewel-like lokum (Turkish delight) in pastel colors of creamy white, yellow, rose, and green. Several varieties had nuts or fruit mixed or rolled into the pectin treat.

The next shop featured baklava, a near eastern pastry made from many layers of paper thin dough, ground nuts, and sugar, and then drenched in a honey syrup. Large round pans filled with varying shapes of the pistachio desert were displayed in front of Ottoman era tiles of cobalt blue and white. Traditional diamond-shaped slices were on the uppermost display, with the more intricate and expensive nest-like confections in the forefront.

An occasional loud announcement shouted by the various vendors assuring that they had the best products was heard over the general hubbub of the crowd.

As well as spices and baklava, Carolyn strolled past stalls selling caviar, dried herbs and tea, apricots, figs, sultana raisins (light golden to dark), prunes, dried mulberries, and sour cherries. Bins of olives, natural green or black, small, medium, large and colossal, plain or stuffed with pimento, pine nuts, or garlic and drenched in olive oil added a thick earthy aroma to the savory mix. Hazelnuts, roasted and blanched, pistachios, almonds, and pine nuts were stacked up in giant sacks with the vendor passing out one or two to all the young children passing by.

Toward the exit of the bazaar was a vendor with large neatly arranged glass jars of every imaginable fruit and vegetable. Whole corn cobs, whole garlic cloves, pickled watermelon chunks, beans, apricots, stuffed roasted red peppers and eggplants were just a few of the items making up the colorful display.

After stepping out of the bazaar on the west side of the market, Carolyn walked toward the outdoor produce stalls selling fresh foodstuff from all over Anatolia.

The open-air area of the market had a wonderful selection of cheeses stacked high where customers indicated the size of chunk they wanted to buy by stretching out their hands.

High rows of boxes leaning back-to-back pyramid style, contained colorful produce: cabbage, tangerines, peppers of every hue, apricots, cilantro, chickpeas on stems, pomegranates, and many

THE KISS GOODNIGHT

things Carolyn had never seen before.

The deep fragrance of coffee, mixed with the heady aroma of nearby cinnamon, clove, fresh mint, and cardamom swirled past her nose as she headed toward a weather-beaten deco building just outside the Spice Market. This was known as the most famous coffee supplier shop in Istanbul, having been in business more than one hundred years.

Stacks of brown wax-paper-wrapped squares of freshly ground coffee lined the walls of the shop where young men sold them nonstop through large open windows. The beans, roasted, and then ground on the premises from morning to night explained the heady fragrance.

Carolyn decided it was time for a coffee break and stepped in line. The rich smell had gotten to her. After ordering a cup of the Turkish coffee that she didn't particularly like, she found an empty seat at a small wrought iron table-for-two next to the large grassy public square. She'd ordered the coffee extra sweet, hoping it would help with the bitterness.

As soon as she sat down, a middle-age Turkish woman sat in the chair across from her. Dressed in shades and patterns, from lilac to mulberry, the colorful flowered scarf that wrapped her head, to her long paisley harem pants, right down to her lavender rubber sandals the woman exuded purple. She had several long ropes of halved and dried red peppers hanging over her shoulder.

"I read your fortune," she said matter-of-factly.

"Oh, no thank-you," Carolyn responded.

She grimaced as she sipped coffee from the edge of the tiny cup.

"Only drink one side, for best fortune," the woman continued. "No two sides."

Realizing it would be more trouble to protest than go along with the impromptu fortune telling, Carolyn acquiesced. As she sipped her coffee, from one side, the woman carried on with a conversation about herself.

In broken English and a smattering of Turkish where she couldn't find the words, Carolyn pieced together a brief history of the purple lady. Apparently, she was the best fortuneteller in the bazaar, and most likely, the whole of Istanbul. Maybe even all of Turkey.

Carolyn was very fortunate already it would appear. She smiled as she listened to the woman, noting the Turkish dialect mixed with English altered between guttural German sounds, to a lilting French melody. After touting her credentials, the sturdy, insistent woman gave her a lesson about the apparent wonders of the coffee she was drinking.

"These beans are roast many times. Many times. Then grind very thin," she said rubbing her hands together back and forth. "Then you cook in cezve. You know cezve?" she asked, making a ladling motion.

Carolyn could tell she was getting frustrated about not knowing the English word for the little brass pot used to boil the coffee. Carolyn didn't know the word either, so she smiled and repeated cezve. The woman nodded, happy that she was understood.

She then continued by making the motion of dropping two spoons full of coffee into the cezve, and then boiling. She said, "Cook," while flexing all ten fingers back and forth around the imaginary cezve. She tried to reenact the motion of dipping a thin layer of foam into two cups. Frustrated again, she proceeded to pour the coffee into the two imaginary cups and finished with a look of "there you have it."

By the time Carolyn finished drinking her cup of coffee, she realized she was getting a jolt of caffeinated energy and found herself appreciating the benefit of Turkish coffee. Doubting it was a taste she would ever crave, still, she'd developed a liking for it.

The woman made a motion with her imaginary cup, indicating that Carolyn should swirl the thick coffee grounds around in the bottom of the cup. After the grounds were sufficiently swirled, the fortuneteller motioned for her to dump the cup upside down on the saucer. She then motioned for her to touch the bottom of the cup with her index finger.

"Extra good luck," she said.

She motioned to turn the cup back up to its normal position in the saucer then took the cup from Carolyn with an impatient "finally" expression.

Now ready for business, she stretched out her arms and legs in her chair causing her strands of dried peppers to fall off her shoulder. As Carolyn stood to help retrieve them, the woman waved her hand across the table.

"Hayir!" she said firmly.

Carolyn assumed that meant no and sat back down. The fortune teller grumbled disgruntled sounds while staring intently into the cup of sludgy grounds. She looked up at Carolyn and jerked her head back and then sideways. She stared at Carolyn for a long moment with a growing fear in her wide eyes and an unmistakable look of distress on her face. She glanced around the table with uneasiness and then shifted her eyes back and forth further out into the crowd.

She stood up, muttering, "Let the future follow your wishes," in a monotone ramble and then hurried away as she looked around the crowd suspiciously. She ambled away looking everywhere but forward while she knocked people out of her way.

Carolyn watched the woman until she disappeared into the tourists and shoppers. She sat there for a moment before picking up the coffee cup. She stared into the grounds looking for some meaning, some reason for such distress, but all she saw were swirls and lumps of fragrant wet bean sediment. She picked up the string of red peppers and hung them on the back of the chair in case the woman came back for them.

"Wow. That was weird," she said, feeling goose bumps creep from the base of her skull down to the back of her arms. She reminded her of Lady Ce'cil.

She glanced around with a slight suspicion at everyone as she walked through the crowd and out of the bustle of the Spice Market. But she saw nothing suspicious in this exotic conglomeration from around the world. Unusual, yes. Suspicious, no.

She'd decided earlier to tour Topkapi Palace. So, with a shrug of her shoulders and a quizzical look still on her face, she stepped outside the market and walked to the first taxi in line at the street. She pointed to the meter to let the taxi driver know she only wanted to pay the legitimate rate. When she realized he understood her by nodding his head in resignation, she got into his cab.

After a short ride, mostly stops and starts with plenty of honking, Carolyn arrived at the cobblestone square just outside the palace's Imperial Gate. Military Gendarme, Turkish armed guards, carrying what looked like AK47s, a common sight around Istanbul, stood guarding the entrance.

Beyond the arched entryway, through the thick stone wall,

buildings of various sizes and shapes surrounded a large park-like setting. Birds chirped as visitors meandered under the shade of ancient trees covering crisscrossed sidewalks and flowerbeds. Carolyn guessed this to be the business quarters of the palace.

Just beyond the ticket booth stood another thick, high wall and arched gateway, allowing access into the residential section of the palace grounds. A parapet lined with the old battlements that the palace guards used as protection spanned the distance between two tall octagonal towers of the gate.

Just inside the gate was another park-like setting. A rococo-styled fountain decorated with intricate tulip tiles from the 1700s graced the entrance to the right. Rows of tall, thick, giant marble columns encircled with gold on the upper and lower rims, greeted visitors as they entered the palace grounds. These massive structures only hinted at the opulence enjoyed by the turbaned sultans, their harems of beautiful concubines, eunuchs, courtiers, and visiting dignitaries for five centuries.

Carolyn made her way to the entrance of the harem pavilion and stood marveling at the intricately tiled ceilings, framed with heavy wood molding.

Gem-colored stained glass windows streamed tinted light onto the large bed-like couches that lined the harem walls. Delicate scrolled window coverings were at the top of each corner of the room. It was rumored to be where the eunuch spies of the concubines sat and listened to gossip. The sprawling marble floors were bare now, but had been covered in luxurious handmade carpets in the days of splendor.

After leaving the harem, Carolyn walked out onto a marble terrace overlooking the Bosphorus. The palace was on the first of The Seven Hills of Old Istanbul on the tip of land jutting out into the strait, surrounded by water on two sides. All seven hills were within the Walls of Constantinople, a defensive brick and limestone wall surrounding the city.

Carolyn remembered learning in school about the Ottoman Age and the earlier Byzantine period. Monumental religious buildings crowned each hill. Churches were built under the Byzantines and Imperial Mosques were built under the Ottomans. The walls, seen throughout the city in various stages of restoration were built in the fourth and fifth centuries.

THE KISS GOODNIGHT

Remembering school made Carolyn think about Sandy. Thoughts of her brother followed right behind.

Don't go there! She admonished herself.

She stood looking out over the water for a long time. Palace intrigue, spying eunuchs and luxury beyond imagination captured her thoughts. She wondered if she would mind being in a harem. Deciding eventually, that she would not, not at all, she headed toward the treasury pavilion. Topkapı's treasury held an incredible collection of objects made of gold, silver, rubies, emeralds, jade, pearls, and diamonds.

The gold and jewel encrusted Sword of Suleiman the Magnificent, encased in a glass box caught her eye.

A good method to deal with the Andrew's of antiquity, no doubt.

In the next display Carolyn found the Topkapı dagger; the palace's most famous exhibit. Three enormous emeralds from the Muzo mines of Columbia decorated its hilt on one side, while diamonds, interspersed between the handle and sheath, decorated the rest of it. An additional octagonal-shaped emerald on the pommel set as a cover, opened to reveal a small watch. Apparently, in case you wanted to check the time you stabbed someone.

The back side of the handle was a combination of mother-of-pearl and an enameled flower motif. The curved blade of the dagger fit smoothly into the curved gold sheath, or so it said on the placard in the case.

But the thing that intrigued Carolyn the most was the gold and diamond studded chain attached to the handle of the dagger. It was the same design as the anklet she'd received from her brother. Carolyn slipped her hand into her bra and pulled out the chain. Yes, it was identical in design, although the chain on the dagger was thinner.

Carolyn slipped her chain back in her bra where she'd been holding it since the incident in the cave. She decided right then to have it repaired at one of the gold shops in the bazaar. Today.

She wondered if her brother had stood in this very spot and gazed upon that dagger. Tears welled up in her eyes and spilled over. She blinked a few times and decided it was time to move on.

The next exhibit was the Kasıkçı Diamond, a teardrop-shaped eighty-six-carat stone. Surrounding the giant stone were dozens of smaller diamonds. The sign said it was a gift to Mehmet IV at his accession to the throne in 1648. It was the fifth largest diamond in the world. Carolyn glanced at it and then walked back to the dagger. She took a deep breath and turned to leave the building.

Carolyn snapped a quick picture of the mosaic tiles lining the walls on her way out. She loved mosaics and tiles but her mood had changed when she saw the dagger chain. The only thing she was interested in now was getting her chain repaired. And maybe one of those Turkish sandwiches.

CHAPTER 18

The exquisitely crafted, jewel-studded Topkapi dagger thrust itself in Carolyn's thoughts as she walked the short distance along the tree-lined boulevard from Topkapi Palace to the Hagia Sophia cathedral.

The thought she might need a dagger began to form in her mind. She'd had enough narrow escapes with Andrew and his thugs to warrant a weapon. Tired of running and not able to carry her pistol anywhere in the Mediterranean, she wondered why she hadn't thought of it before now.

The sun, in its attempt to peek from the low-lying clouds hugging the Golden Horn, glinted on the windows high above on the massive dome of Hagia Sophia. The flash drew Carolyn's attention as she walked to the edge of the square to catch another taxi.

She stepped over to a taxi and pointed to the meter, again with a firm expression. The taxi driver looked over at her, bobbed his head up in the air, raised his eyebrows, and clicked his tongue. She took this as a no and walked to the next taxi. As she walked away, the driver got out of his cab and called to her, "Bayan, bayan, my taxi, yes?"

But she'd had enough of dealing with difficult people. Even if she had to start with taxi drivers, she'd decided it was time to stand her ground. That dagger had given her a renewed courage. She wasn't sure why. It might have been the dagger chain.

"Gold shops, bazaar," she told the second, more agreeable taxi driver. After a little reading in a guidebook, Carolyn had learned that the Grand Bazaar covered over seventy-five acres and housed over 3,000 shops. Even though her leg was feeling better, the thought of walking the entire bazaar looking for gold shops was daunting.

After giving the taxi driver a generous tip she headed for the first order of business. A sandwich. She was starving.

A streak of sunlight streamed in the high set windows on each side of the vaulted Byzantium arched ceiling. The crisscrossed ambient light dappled on the red Turkish flags that hung at the entrance of every shop down the long hallway. Copper and silver pots and trays displayed in the passage reflected the random sun rays. It took a moment to adjust her eyes to the dim light of the cavernous building.

She walked down one of the main thoroughfares following her nose. The smell of roasting meat was coming from somewhere and she resolved to find it in this maze of shops.

She turned down the first corridor to the right. The walkway filled with bins of trinkets, hand-painted plates, and colorful round lanterns dangled from the walls as far down into the corridor as she could see. But she'd lost the aroma, so she turned back.

In the corridor to the left, she picked up the aroma again. An awning over the front of the establishment and the clatter of dishes inside told her she was in the right place. As she stepped in, the waiter took her order and directed her to a seat at a long trough-like table near the open kitchen. The portly, mustached cook stood grilling strips of meat on long metal skewers with brass handles bearing the likeness of different animal figures. From where she sat, most the handles appeared to be lambs.

A large trough between her table and the kitchen overflowed with fresh dill, cilantro, sliced tomatoes, lemons, onions, and garlic cloves. Open glass bowls containing different colored spices lined up next to the grill. The cook took a pinch from the nearest bowl and sprinkled it over the grilling meat, then lifted a five-gallon metal container and drizzled the spiced meat with olive oil. The grill sizzled carrying the meat and herb aroma throughout the small crowded room and out into the bazaar. Carolyn's mouth watered. Several small mountains of flatbread stacked against the tile wall behind the spice bowls were handy when the cook got an order. With a nod from the waiter he would grab a flatbread and place it on top of two skewers of meat, wait a moment then flip it. The waiter appeared again, as if my magic, with a square sheet of paper. He squeezed the seared meat off the skewers with the paper-wrapped bread and dressed the contents with items from the trough. After a generous sprinkling of sumac, a tangy lemon-flavored ground red berry, and two quick dollops of yogurt he then expertly rolled it.

It was in her hand and he'd hurried away to seat the next incoming patron before she could say thank you.

As she bit into the soft warm bread, she caught the eye of the cook. He nodded his head up and down with no expression as if he bounced to his internal rhythm while he awaited approval. She smiled and nodded back. He nodded and then turned back to work continuing to nod.

The strong taste of garlic mixed with the fresh cilantro and lemon with dill yogurt sauce had Carolyn gobbling the sandwich. She noticed other diners gobbling their sandwiches, so she dispensed with etiquette and just enjoyed. The garlicky dill sauce was running down her wrist by the time she'd eaten her fill. She had to use four napkins to clean up and smelled like garlic the rest of the day. But it was worth it. With her first objective in Istanbul accomplished, eating a Turkish sandwich, she was ready to forge on to repair the chain.

The bazaar was more like a small city than any shopping mall she'd ever seen back home. Even though she'd been dropped off near the gold streets, she ended up walking through endless alleyways that crisscrossed through an occasional unexpected courtyard. She sat down at the rim of an ancient fountain in the middle of one courtyard to take a break and consult the little paper map she'd picked up at the entrance.

After figuring out where she was and where she needed to go, she sat with her eyes closed, just wanting to listen to the sounds of the bazaar. A bell clanged somewhere far off at an ice cream stall. A child was crying because he'd gotten no ice cream, no doubt. She could hear footsteps on the ancient stone floor, salesmen calling out their wares, laughter and the low hum of conversation. With her chin cocked up and her head tilted back to better appreciate the sounds of the bazaar, Carolyn opened her eyes.

Light from the windows curved into the arches of the vaulted ceiling above her, highlighting the blue arabesques that decorated the yellow plaster. Even the ceiling in the grand bazaar was remarkable and grand.

After gaining her bearings, Carolyn moved past the shops filled with fancy dishware and ceramic plates of every color and design that lined windows and shelves. She heard an earnest shopkeeper trying to explain, in his broken English the Turkish reason for the different color teacups to an Aussie shopper. A large orange tabby cat napping on a bin of glass evil-eye beads invited shoppers to purchase baskets and wooden utensils of every imaginable use.

Two women dressed in traditional abaya, black chiffon robe-like caftans that covered everything but a strip for their eyes, were haggling with a shopkeeper over an onyx chess set. Carolyn wondered how they would manage to carry away the heavy stone chessboard if they were to negotiate a price. She stopped for a moment, admiring the white carved marble chess pieces on one side and deep caramel shaded pieces on the opposing side.

As she watched this playing out, a handsome man in an impeccable suit walked by. It was obvious he was all about style, as he kept his chic sunglasses on despite the dimness of the bazaar.

Carolyn watched him walk off, smiling at how self-obsessed he was, remembering how silly she'd been for falling for Andrew's many similar performances.

She continued through the crowd, passing shops that contained more than she could ever imagine. Leather, fabric, carpet, mosaic glass globes reflecting a rainbow of colors from minuscule mirrors, water pipes, and handmade mandolin shops each had young boys darting expertly through the crowds carrying trays with complimentary glasses of hot tea.

Carolyn stopped in front of one window displaying meerschaum pipes. Artisans found the creamy-white, soft stone easy to carve making it perfect for designing the intricate pipes. Her brother had sent her one with an eagle clawing the pipe bowl a year ago.

No, it'd been longer than that, she remembered.

A loud scream came from the shop two doors down followed by an instant racket. Carolyn looked over to see a crowd gather around a woman and a young man of about seventeen. The woman shrieked at him as he stood with his head hanging. As she continued

THE KISS GOODNIGHT

yelling, some of the other shoppers chimed in. In a matter of moments, two military Gendarme had hold of him. As they led him away, the crowd chanted "thief" and "hirsiz."

Carolyn asked the shopper next to her what happened.

"Thief!" the lady said indignantly. "He steal. He should have hands cut off, like old way!"

With that she clicked her tongue and walked off. Carolyn stood there until the crowd dispersed. She was a little surprised at the crowd's reaction, even though she knew minor crimes here received harsh punishment, by American standards.

She continued following the labyrinth toward the gold streets indicated on the map but not sure how she'd gotten so far off course. Once she turned the corner on the major gold thoroughfare, more gold than she ever knew existed on Earth shined through windows and down the street as far as she could see.

These gold shops, unlike most of the other shops, had windows, doors, locks, and safes too, for obvious reasons. Shop owner after shop owner called from their doorways beckoning tourists, touting the best prices. Their voices echoed down the corridors.

She continued walking by the shops, passing the ones calling out to her.

As she approached one shop, the shopkeeper nodded and gave her a polite smile. As she walked toward him, he bowed and opened the door. She got a good vibe from him and stepped inside.

"I need a repair," she told him.

"Oh, you come to best repair. My uncle, he best fix in all city," the young man said confidently, without being arrogant. Carolyn smiled skeptically, thinking how extraordinary her luck was, once again.

"Uncle Kubilay? I have fix for you!" he yelled into the back room.

Carolyn turned to the corner of the shop, away from the counter to retrieve her chain from her bra. She set it down on the black velvet tray.

"Oh, is nice one," said Uncle Kubilay, coming from behind the curtain of his workroom. He picked up the delicate chain to examine it. When he got to the clasp, a quizzical look spread over his face.

"Is splendid. But this, this not good. This ugly," he said, tapping the clasp with his tool.

Carolyn smiled at his frankness.

She'd always thought the size of the clasp was a bit too large for the delicate gold and diamonds too, but the inscription was so meaningful and beautiful. She felt it was her brother's message from beyond the grave telling her to look inside of herself for the strength he'd always told her was there. And she'd found she needed reminding of that often since he passed away.

"What this say?" asked Uncle Kubilay.

"Follow your heart. Look within," Carolyn recited to him with a proud, poetic lilt.

"What inside?" he asked, tapping on the clasp.

Carolyn slowly shook her head back and forth.

"No. Nothing's inside. It means look inside your heart," she said in a kind tone, much as you would when correcting a child.

"No, something inside. This why so big. So ugly."

Carolyn was beginning to doubt her choice in picking this gold shop. In fact, she was thinking, must I always choose the wrong person?

The shopkeeper tapped on the clasp again and said, "I open, see inside."

"There IS nothing inside. It's in your heart," she said patting her hand over her heart.

Uncle Kubilay slid the black velvet tray holding the chain under his loop stand and pulled out a tiny pin-like blade.

"I fix ugly clasp like new after see inside," he said.

Before she could protest, he had popped it open. Fitting perfectly inside the clasp was a tiny green piece of plastic. A boring conversation where her brother spoke about electronic circuits, semiconductor material and diodes zoomed through her mind. Carolyn recognized the small green piece of plastic as a microchip.

"Seeee?" Uncle Kubilay said matter-of-factly.

Carolyn stood with her mouth open.

CHAPTER 19

Carolyn kept standing with her mouth open as Uncle Kubilay picked up the chain and headed to the back room. She wasn't sure how long he'd been back there, but it hadn't been long. Uncle Kubilay darted glances toward Carolyn, watching for further reaction as he worked. He put the small chip back in the clasp and hurried to finish the repair. With a look of genuine compassion on his face, he stepped from behind the counter and put the chain in her outstretched palm. He covered her delicate, shaking hand with both of his and held it firm.

"Is splendid chain, Bayon. Splendid," he said.

Carolyn gazed at him with no expression as a tear welled above her eyelid. Motionless, but for the slight gathering of saline, they stood facing one another until the tear breached the confines of its temporary holding cell and tumbled down her cheek.

"Mustaf! Where is Bayan's tea?" shouted the uncle.

The nephew had been watching the exchange in as much surprise as Carolyn until his uncle's sharp inquiry jolted him to action.

He mumbled and ran out of the shop.

"How much?" Carolyn asked.

"Is my pleasure, Bayan. My pleasure," he said.

"Thanks," Carolyn replied as she walked out of the shop. Without a thought for modesty, she reached in her shirt and put the chain back in her bra.

Uncle Kubilay stood at the doorway watching as Carolyn walked away. He shook his head when Carolyn looked back at him.

She knew what he was thinking, even in his accent.

How she didn't know? So ugly.

As if in the trance of a nightmare, Carolyn walked the equivalent of a city block. Her mind refused to function. The many sounds of the bazaar she'd been enjoying earlier were muted and far off, as if she were slogging through a tunnel. She slowed to a stop and then leaned her forehead against the cool glass of a shop window and closed her eyes.

Tears filled her eyes as she wondered what had just happened and why it had made her cry. The lump grew in her throat as her thoughts floated in confusion. Her legs trembled and grew weak. What was she was doing there? She stood wavering in the grand hallway of the gold bazar and wished she were back on her yacht where she could think.

When her eyes dragged open again, she noticed a small spotlight gleaming a sharp beam upon a snake rapier bracelet in the window display.

The burnished silver snake eyes glowered at her as they reflected light from the chandelier suspended above. Intricately carved scales slinking down the length of the body to slither around its own tail embellished the sinister jewelry.

The snake's head and neck, attached to a thin, sharp blade was partially extracted for display. Later, she didn't remember what she'd paid for it, or any conversation about it. She could only recall the resonance of scraping metal-on-metal and the hum of the sharp thin blade as she pushed and pulled its head, repeatedly drawing out the blade.

Carolyn, still in a daze, walked to the boulevard to catch a taxi. Peeking from beneath her sleeve was the permanent scowl of a silver reptilian bangle.

She opened the door and stepped into the first taxi in line. She didn't eye the meter. She didn't insinuate that she would only pay the fair price.

"Hotel Sultana, 171 Cengelkoy Caddesi," she said.

Carolyn leaned her head away from the faded fringe bric-a-brac lining the back window of the cab and closed her eyes.

Everything blurred. Noise, traffic, her thoughts. Everything.

She rubbed the nubby scales of the snake sword with the tip of her fingers and wished she were back on The Kiss Goodnight where she could think.

The car came to a stop, and the driver rolled down the window to pay the bridge toll.

She realized she should've taken the ferry back as she saw the traffic building. It was rush hour now, and this would take forever.

Nothing she could do about it now, she thought, and closed her eyes again.

The traffic crawled over the bridge as the pink haze of twilight rose from beneath the earth to embrace the landscape in a deceptive innocent blush.

Usually her favorite time of day, on this day Carolyn longed for the quiet, empty blackness of night where she could see through secrets and lies. She longed for that morose place she'd always run from as she preferred the illusions of glowing daylight. Unearthing the painful memories of dark reality was a place to avoid, she'd always thought.

But she needed that place now. She needed to concentrate.

Her mind raced as fast as the spectrum of changing color that dashed across the sky. Hushed violet tones scattered while vibrant pinks emerged from behind the tall buildings and minarets looming on the skyline.

Carolyn pressed harder on the nubby scales of the snake fearing that she might lose touch with reality if she didn't hold onto something.

The subconscious mantra, I need The Kiss Goodnight, I have to get back there, permeated her thoughts like an earworm.

For reasons she didn't understand, she resented the beauty of the vibrant bands on the horizon churling from pink to orange. She closed her eyes again and waited for darkness.

A crunching collision on the left fender behind Carolyn's seat jerked the car to a stop. She turned to see a large dark vehicle with blackened windows as it backed up and revved the engine. The deep rattling grumble of the motor shook the sinister auto as it readied for another charge.

Carolyn sat helpless as an ear-splitting shriek and a cloud of noxious smoke belched from the tires. A panicked low-pitched curse roared from the driver as he shouted and waved his hand. The second hit caused the car to crash into the bridge rail. Carolyn sat stunned as she watched a tall man limp at a fast pace toward her taxi. A static of thoughts jolted through her mind before she recognized that it was Andrew.

Carolyn watched the scene as if in slow motion, wondering that she had no control of the shrill scream escaping her throat. The car door swung open and Andrew reached in and jerked her arm. She tumbled out of the car. The protesting driver tried to open his door, but it had been pushed in by the crash. He fumbled to the other side of the car, but the bridge pinned in that door, as well.

With her feet only skimming the ground, Andrew dragged Carolyn to the side of the bridge.

"You have wasted a lot of my time, you fucking little bitch."

As if this were happening in slow motion, Carolyn looked at Andrew's scowling face.

He wasn't even trying to hide his snarl, she thought with a disconnected amusement.

"Where the fuck is it?" Andrew screamed.

"I don't know, Andrew," she said, twisting her neck under his hand. "Where's what?"

"The chain, you fool. Your brother's chain!"

In that split second, thoughts of the bayou, the ransacking, the microchip, all came together in a spinning vortex to rip away every shred of previous reality she'd had about Andrew.

"I lost it in the cave," she cried.

Andrew glared at her as he tried to discern if she was telling the truth.

He screamed, "Damn! That's what I figured. You know, Carolyn, you're as naïve and ignorant as I always thought you were. And your asshole brother, so honorable, so patriotic, was nothing more than a fucking government patsy. The price of his nobility was his death. And now yours. How fitting that you will join him here, right where he died," he said as he dug his fingernails into her throat and dragged her to a cross beam on the bridge railing.

People sat frozen, staring from their cars. One or two looked around as if maybe they should get involved.

THE KISS GOODNIGHT

"My brother?" she coughed.

"Yes, your brother. The motherfucker shot me in the hip. Piss poor aim," he said with a laugh.

"Although, considering he was falling to his death at the time, I guess he wasn't all that bad."

Andrew tightened the grip on Carolyn's throat as he bent her back over the bridge railing.

"It's a shame to kill you Carolyn. You are so beautiful. And you gave me a serious run for my money. Much slyer than those CIA and Interpol bastards. If you weren't such a pathetically good person, we might have even worked together. What about one last kiss good night? he said as he rolled his head back in laughter, trying to get in a final dig.

The sun blazed a bloody orange, lighting the sky as if it had opened the portal to hell. A golden pall cast down on the bridge causing Andrew's perfectly highlighted hair to reflect in a sickening tinge of green as Carolyn slid the blade from her delicately engraved silver bracelet. She balanced her back on the bridge, steadying her hips between the bars. All the training and working out with her brother, keeping him company while he kept fit for the CIA, came to her now instinctively.

As Andrew lowered his head from his hearty laugh, Carolyn looked him straight in the eye. A moment of confusion, then fear washed across his ashen face as she plunged the razor-sharp blade into the stubbled fleshy skin between the sinews of his neck. At that same moment her knee landed a groin-crushing blow into Andrew's only softness. His face contorted into the ugly monster he was as he gasped and lost his balance.

Carolyn gripped her arms tight around the railing and using both legs, swept his feet out from under him. The force of the push caused her to fall to the pavement as he flipped over the railing.

Andrew fell down, straight down, winding his arms around like one of those waving wind dancers that blow wildly in front of cheap used car lots before he splashed into the water, feet first.

Carolyn was back on her feet before anyone from the gathering crowd made it to her. She looked down at the bloody blade and slipped it back into the snake sheath with a slick, firm push.

As people rushed toward her, Carolyn took a deep breath. She held up her chin and began walking through the stopped cars and rushing crowd back to the entrance of the bridge. One Turkish lady grabbed her sleeve and tried to pull her back to the scene. She spoke excited words Carolyn didn't understand.

Carolyn flared her nostrils and widened her eyes. She leaned her face and shoulders toward the woman.

"NO!" she growled in a voice she hadn't known she'd possessed. The lady let go of her sleeve and stepped back. The few others that had gathered took a step back as well.

Snarled traffic kept the police from getting to the scene. In a moment of panic, she stopped and peered over the bridge, making sure he wasn't down there swimming. She saw nothing but dark swirling water. A military-style boat from the side of the bridge headed for the spot where he'd fallen in.

How unfortunate. He'll have drowned by the time they make it, if the fall didn't kill him. Or the stab, Carolyn thought with a smile.

"Fuck Andrew," she said. "I'm going home."

THE KISS GOODNIGHT

CHAPTER 20

After finding her gate in the cavernous and confusing Ataturk airport in Istanbul, Carolyn purchased a few things while waiting for her flight out to Malta. She never went back to her hotel. Nor did she stop to talk to the police.

As far as she was concerned, it was over. Andrew was dead. And she was happy about it. In fact, she was so happy about it, she almost felt guilty. But no, she couldn't feel guilty. She was glad she'd killed him. Recalling the surprised look on his face as she pulled the blade from her wrist and drove it into his throat made her smile. It would be her "happy place" for a long time.

After arriving in Malta, it didn't take long before she had to close her eyes and conjure up that happy place in her mind once again. The joy at seeing The Kiss Goodnight was quickly replaced with forcing herself to think about Andrew's expression again. It was obvious he'd been there while she was in Istanbul. Everything had been tossed and broken.

She thought of Lady Ce'cil and about how she cackled after describing her dearly departed husband's agonized face while being eaten by an alligator. She could relate. Carolyn tried to cackle a few times and then laughed at her sad attempt. Even though her yacht was ransacked, Andrew was dead. Nothing could take that relief away from her. At least her mast had been repaired. And much sooner and cheaper than expected. Overall, Carolyn was pleased.

She plotted her course, this time up through the Strait of Messina, the narrow passageway between the Island of Sicily and the toe of Italy's boot.

"No worries about anyone trying to find me there this time," she said with another lame attempt at a cackle.

She spent the evening straightening things and then headed for the chandlery for supplies and to pay the last of the dock fee. The trip home to Portofino and Augie's vineyard, the only place she felt at home anymore, or maybe ever, would take about a week of sailing. But she felt good. Her leg was healing nicely, albeit with a horrible jagged scar, and she'd eaten and rested quite well in Istanbul. Still humming with adrenaline, she knew this was the time to go home.

"We returned your coin under the mast, Miss Wingate. It's a nice one. The bee from Ephesus," the harbor master told her. "Just in case."

"Coin?" she asked.

"Yes, your payment to that old demon Charon, the ferryman who will take you across the river Styx if anything happens to you while you're on your yacht. If you don't pay the fee, your soul would be doomed to wander the Earth forever. Shipwrights have done this for thousands of years," he said in that way that was almost incredulous, but not quite.

The only thing she could think to say was, "Oh, thank you."

At dawn the next morning, Carolyn was at the helm motoring out of the marina. Once she cleared the dock and last buoy marking the entrance, she untied the sails and raised the jib, main, and mizzen and then shut off the engine. After adjusting the sails somewhat, she was soon slicing through the two-foot waves at a slick pace of about six knots heading north, northwest.

Carolyn let out a loud whoop and lifted her face into the fresh morning air as the bow, crashing through the waves, thrilled her pulse. She would think about all the things Andrew had said to her while at anchor later tonight.

But right now she sailed. As the wind grabbed the sheets and pulled her through the sea, she felt powerful. She'd never felt so powerful in her life

Despite deciding to think about Andrew's words at anchor that night, she couldn't bring herself to do it. Instead, after anchoring, she straightened some of the supplies Andrew had thrown around and then rested by the helm. Keeping one eye on the sail trim and the other on watch, she tried to read a Stephen King novel. She caught tiny catnaps here and there between chapters.

In the afternoon of the fourth day a scratching static buzzed from her radio.

"Kiss Goodnight," she answered.

Crackling static answered back. After repeating this three times, she heard a word that sent a shiver up her spine:

Augie.

"What about Augie?" she begged. "What about Augie?"

More scratching continued until it quit altogether.

Damned Andrew had destroyed her radio.

She decided to sail the rest of the way without stopping to anchor.

A few loud flaps of the sail brought Carolyn out of the dead stare state she'd been in, since the radio crackled out the word Augie.

What could it be?' she kept wondering. He's never radioed me before.

Lost in thought, Carolyn hadn't noticed the wind dying down and The Kiss Goodnight rolling in the waves. She flipped on the engine. Keeping the mainsail up, she motor-sailed into the slight breeze at an angle, tacking every so often along the way.

She kept the main sail on the centerline and flattened it as much as possible, keeping the wind angle tight and the sail filled. Successful with this tactic, she put a little more shape in the sail and rolled out the jib, causing the yacht to glide through the water faster. Even The Kiss Goodnight was eager to get home.

Carolyn wasn't sure when day had passed into night as she woke and jumped to her feet. It was dangerous to sail long stretches alone, especially with as little experience as she had. After searching 360 degrees around the yacht and finding no sign of light from land or any other ships, she sighed with relief. She was alone in an empty sea.

Stretching across the night sky, trillions of stars not only lit the sky, but also highlighted the vastness of the universe and the smallness of her life. A hazy band of white light cascaded outward in a wide arch across the horizon. Interstellar dust, gasses, and stars made up the Milky Way, or river of milk, as the ancients referred to it. Carolyn gazed into it, allowing her mind to float in the darkness, somewhere between heaven and the sea. She lost herself to the majesty.

Flashes of phosphorescent light caused by tiny sea animals glittering in her path, twinkled from the bow spray as the yacht forged on through the magical blackness.

She allowed herself to remember the hazy moon and the glittering sea on the night she'd first invited Griff aboard The Kiss Goodnight. She felt an ache in her heart when she pictured his face and realized how much she missed him. The green flash in his eyes. His laugh.

Oh well, she had more important things to think about now. And even those things were packed and stored away in the attic of her mind, as surely as her mother would pack away her summer clothes to prepare for winter.

No coincidence that her clothes were packed and stored in the attic with Rawhead and Bloody Bones, just as her thoughts were stored in the attic of her mind with Andrew.

CHAPTER 21

Carolyn arrived in Portofino midmorning after the sixth day of sailing. Exhausted, but not able to rest until she found out why Augie had radioed her, she took a quick shower and lowered her dinghy to head for the dock. The marina was empty except for a few tourists. Even Ramone was gone. She tied up the dinghy and walked to the Vespa stand. There was no one there, either. She waited, pacing and looking around for five minutes before scrawling a note and taking the key to the Vespa she usually used from under the makeshift wooden counter. A few months ago, she would never have done such a thing. Probably not even a week ago, before Andrew's death. But now, things were different. She was different. She hopped onto the little motorbike and headed up the hill out of town.

Her heart pounded as the tall cypress trees lining Augie's drive to the vineyard came into view. When she was close enough to see the large stone and stucco house and the bench where Augie and Ombra always sat waiting for her, she whimpered. No one was there.

As she pushed harder on the throttle, she looked between the rows of grapevines hoping to find Augie stooped while working the vines. A pile of long empty baskets in one row, about ten feet in from the drive, caused her to screech on the brakes.

Maybe Augie fell?

The bike skidded in the soft, dirt-gravel road and Carolyn's knee and elbow scraped into a bloody mess. Realizing it was only a pile of baskets, she picked up the bike and with a groan, she hopped on again. She gunned it the rest of the way to the house.

She turned off the engine and stood there, looking for a sign, any sign, of Augie.

A loud clang from behind Augie's house caused the trees to explode in a thick veil of midnight black crows as they scattered in the cloudless sky. The loud flap and flutter of their screeching, raspy caws as they rallied together their mob caused Carolyn to head in that direction. She followed the clanging bell past the back of the house to a grassy path that led to a small stand of trees at the top of the hill.

The sound grew louder as the bell continued to toll. One, two, three rings. As she got closer to the sound, she heard the muffled voice of someone talking. Four, five, six rings. She started to run.

From the top of the hill, she looked down into a small hollow to see a crowd of people sitting outside a small, ancient two-story chapel. Augie had never mentioned a church on the property. But why would he? He wasn't a particularly religious man. It looked to be a remnant from the centuries old convent. As she rushed closer, the bell rang the seventh and final time from what she could now see was a tall thin bell tower behind the convent.

A few people in the back row turned around.

"Augie?" she cried out softly.

She recognized a few faces from town as she stood at the back of the small crowd. Her dirty face and bloody leg caused them to look at her with surprise. No one made a sound.

"Augie?" Carolyn whimpered again.

She looked from face to face as she searched on either side of the aisle. Everyone continued to stare as she walked up between the rows of folding chairs.

A vague realization hit Carolyn as she noticed a casket resting in the doorway of the chapel. Ombra lay beneath it.

Her head jerked back in horror and disbelief.

Before she could fully grasp the meaning of the casket, a dark-haired man in the front row stood up and turned around. When Carolyn recognized him, her eyes closed. She was back on The Kiss Goodnight, weightless, falling and floating at the same time, up into the stars from the night before as her knees buckled and she plummeted into the merciful white blur of unconsciousness.

THE KISS GOODNIGHT

After a moment, she opened her eyes. Tomas was next to her with his arms draped around her. She could hear him calling to her from the fog. She closed her eyes again.

Tomas reached around her back and legs and carried her to the house. He set her in the chair she'd always used on the veranda. Tomas sat in Augie's chair.

Carolyn drifted in and out of a fog as she came to realize Augie was gone. She leaned her forehead over her folded arms and began to sob.

Tomas held her arm.

"Ramone, make her some coffee, please. And add some Grappa," Tomas said. "It should be in the cabinet on the left of the sink."

Carolyn looked up in confusion.

"Augie is my father, Carolyn. *Was* my father," he corrected himself.

Carolyn put her head back in her arms and sobbed again. After several minutes she lifted her head again.

"What happened?" she asked

"Someone shot him. Near a week ago. He was roughed up pretty bad, too. He held on for days. He wanted to see you. I tried to call. I didn't realize the Carolyn he was trying to see was you, the same Carolyn I'd met at Bue Marino."

"Who shot him?" Carolyn asked, with a horrifying feeling she already knew.

"We can talk about that later. I need to get back to the chapel. Ramone, take her upstairs so she can lie down. I'll be back soon. We'll talk," he said.

"Ramone, you go with Tomas, I'll be fine," Carolyn said.

Carolyn sat numb, staring out over the vineyard to the ocean until the guests started coming back over the hill.

Much like a zombie she'd seen in the popular movie advertisements; she picked up her coffee, climbed the stairs to the bathroom, and grabbed a towel. She would have to shower later. She went to one of the spare rooms, spread the towel on the bed and lay down. She'd been awake for most of the last week, sleeping only in catnaps. She gripped the side of the bed as she closed her eyes. Between the spinning and the rushing noise in her ears, she felt like she was still riding waves. Exhaustion and Grappa finally claimed her. She fell asleep.

CHAPTER 22

Somewhere, way back in her mind, in a tiny locked and forgotten hidey-hole, a disturbance was rustling about. Her heart thumped louder with each slow step as she walked toward the low, weathered doorway. Blood rushing through her ears drowned out every other sound as she reached for the door handle. Her own low, guttural groan woke her at the same moment the giant disembodied dog nose pushed its way through the opening door.

She opened her eyes to pitch blackness.

"Where am I?"

It took a moment for her eyes to adjust before she saw the stars through the window.

A long, mournful wail ending in a pitiful, plaintive howl from the woods behind the house reminded her she was at the vineyard.

And that Augie was gone.

The wailing howl continued.

That heart-wrenching sound must have caused the disturbing dream.

She made her way, still foggy from her nightmare, to the kitchen to make coffee. A small light flickered from a candle on the veranda. Tomas sat staring into the predawn darkness. She joined him and set down her coffee. Neither of them said a word. They listened.

As the sun rose, the reflected sound waves of the dreadful

howl no longer sounded earthly. It was unsettling. A last loud wail lingered through the valley before it ceased.

Tomas went to the kitchen and returned with a fresh cup of coffee for each of them.

"Carolyn," he began.

"Andrew killed my father."

Carolyn sat quietly.

"You knew Andrew. Your brother knew Andrew." he said sharply, as the muscle in his cheek rippled up and down from his clenching jaw.

"He tried to kill you. He did kill your brother."

Carolyn took a deep breath.

"Yes. I just found …" she said trailing off in midsentence, noticing for the first time the dry blood crusted on the face of the snake rapier still dangling around her wrist. She covered it with her other hand and pulled her arm to her side.

"Andrew is a black market arms dealer, Carolyn. Making millions trafficking weapons to Africa and the Middle East," he said.

"I didn't know," Carolyn said.

"I had no idea at all."

"Why do you think he is trying to kill you, then? He suspected your brother sent you a list of his contacts. Your brother was the only agent ever able to get close to him," he said.

"When he found out he was on to him, he wasted no time killing him. He's ruthless, Carolyn. Surely you know that?"

"I do know that," she said while lowering her head.

"Did you know my brother?" Her voice quivered.

"No. But we knew of each other. Agencies from around the globe have been watching Andrew for years. He began his billion-dollar business touring Europe for old weapons to use in Hollywood productions. He managed to turn his failed commercial shipping and air cargo companies into one of the single most lucrative businesses in the world. Gunrunning."

Over the next several hours, Carolyn learned quite a bit about Andrew. Not the Armani-clad, globetrotting socialite he portrayed himself to be, but rather, he was one of the most successful arms dealers in the world, keeping trigger-happy Jihadists, revolutionaries, and dictators happy by supplying them with sophisticated weapons.

THE KISS GOODNIGHT

Carolyn sat stunned as Tomas recounted a staggering list of countries and weapons deals. Surface-to-air missiles bought in Russia, sold to Ukraine. Stingers from Pakistan at $80,000 a pop, sold to Afghanistan.

Warlords and dictators from Ukraine and Moldova, throughout the Middle East and on to Nigeria, Gaza, Liberia, and Sudan in Africa, had been on a nickname basis with him. They'd call him Brown-Brown because of his habit of snorting a double line of cocaine mixed with gunpowder at the completion of each deal. The smokeless gunpowder, containing nitroglycerin, a drug prescribed for heart conditions because it increases blood flow, allows the cocaine to move more freely through the body.

On the east coast of Africa he is known as "Death Stalker" after a particularly nasty scorpion, for arming Somalia Islamists that killed more than five-thousand people in Somalia and Kenya.

All in all, Andrew had supplied handguns, AK-47s, heavy machine guns, flamethrowers, rocket-propelled grenades, and surface-to-air missiles. He sold Semtex, an odorless explosive invisible to X-rays and many times more powerful than fertilizer, to seven of the top ten war zones in the world.

"Are you sure?" Carolyn asked. "Are you sure it was Andrew? He seemed so… I don't know. Lazy."

"Yes, Carolyn. He has even armed revolutionaries that would happily kill Americans. His own countrymen, Carolyn! His own countrymen!

And now he has killed my father. He was looking for you, for the information your brother may have sent you," he said as he looked away from her and winced.

"He must be stopped. He must be killed. As soon as he we locate him, I will kill him myself."

For the first time in days, Carolyn found a smile welling up inside her. She put her face in her bent elbow, not wanting Tomas to think her insensitive and pictured Andrew's face as she sharply thrust the long thin blade into his neck. The thought of his atrocities replaced the smile with nausea. She ran to the bathroom.

Tomas put away his phone as she returned to the table.

"I have to leave. You can stay here as long as you like, Carolyn. I have people in town watching the dock. And Old Man

Paganelli, who lives about four miles down the road, is an ex-carabinier. He's heavily armed, and he's watching the house. You'll be safe here. And by the way, I don't know why you ran away from your friend, Griff, but he was only trying to help you."

Carolyn nodded, already knowing she'd be safe. Andrew was dead.

She sat on the veranda the rest of the day, trying to absorb what she'd learned about Andrew, Tomas, and Griff until she noticed the approach of twilight creep over the ocean. She went to the kitchen. She didn't want to see anything lovely.

She cut two thick slabs of bread from a loaf on the counter and then went to the refrigerator to see what was there. Guests from the ceremony had filled it. She pulled out a large plate of fried chicken cutlets and a bowl of green salad with small ring-shaped tubetinni and chunks of peperoni. After spooning a heap of salad on one slab of bread and a chicken cutlet on the other, she mashed them together, grabbed a bottle of wine, and sat down. Four bites of the sandwich and she was finished, but she continued drinking the wine. She sat in the living room drinking wine and staring into the empty fireplace the rest of the evening.

As the last trace of light disappeared from the sky, the howling began again. Carolyn took a deep breath and headed for the shower. She was filthy. Crusted blood still clung to her leg and dust still covered her face. She stood in the shower until the water ran cold. Then she rinsed out her clothes and hung them to dry. Wearing only a towel, she went to Augie's room to see if he had any clothes she could wear.

Odd that she hadn't cried about his death when that's all she did when her brother passed away.

In Augie's closet, she found a well-worn plaid shirt that hung to her knees. In looking through his dresser drawers for some pants or shorts, she came across an old leather-bound album. She carried the heavy book to Augie's bed and climbed up the two steps to get onto the high mattress, then sat back on a fluffy stack of feather pillows. Augie's wife must have set up this soft, comfortable bed. Augie was generally a man of simple tastes, unless it came to his yacht, of course.

Ombra's wailing and howling from the chapel caused Carolyn to climb back down and shut the door.

THE KISS GOODNIGHT

Poor Ombra. If he hadn't come home by morning, she'd take him some food and water.

She lit a fire in the small fireplace and climbed back onto the big bed.

I'll go back to the guest room when Ombra quits yowling, she told herself.

The first page in the album was a large, black-and-white photo of a much younger Augie and his beautiful dark haired bride. He looked so happy, so full of life.

And he was gone now, because of her, she thought.

She turned the page.

Page after page showed Augie and his family, the vineyard, and the yacht. He'd lived a good life. He had a good wife and two good sons.

"I wonder why he was so angry with them?" she wondered aloud.

Toward the end of the album was a certificate from Sapienza University of Rome with the name Augustine Aliberti Jr. M.D. inscribed in calligraphy. Augie's first-born son. Between the last page of the album and the worn leather binding was a sheaf of certificates with the heading, AISE, External Information and Security Agency. The name Tomas Aliberti was written on each certificate.

"Recognition for Commemorative Cross for operations in Afghanistan, Medal of Meritorious Service, Cross for Valor and Star of Merit," she read aloud. But she stopped when she saw the Sniper Elite award.

"Tomas!" she said. "Of course. He shot Bug."

She looked up from the album and remembered that night. Slipping away from a sleeping Griff, the sound of the shot reverberating off the volcano, the terror, motoring out of the marina in the dark, it all came back to her as if it'd happened last night. It hadn't happened last night though. Last night was the night Augie spent the first night of forever in his grave.

Carolyn closed the album and went to the guest room.

That dog! she thought. *That dog!*

She pulled the pillow tight over her ears.

The next morning, after coffee and a slice of bread with honey, she got busy cleaning Augie's kitchen. At first glance, it looked orderly and clean. But after looking around a little, she noticed a layer of dust and grime in the cabinets and on the back of the counters. She grabbed a bucket and began scrubbing. She enjoyed doing the busy work. It kept her mind clear. When the toothpick broke she was using to clean dust from between the trim molding around the living room floor, Carolyn noticed the house had darkened as the sun began to set. It was late afternoon already, and she'd forgotten to take Ombra food and water.

She'd do it tomorrow, she thought. But as she poured herself a glass of wine, she remembered his agonizing howl.

"Damn," she mumbled.

She grabbed a bottle of water, a few chicken cutlets, and a bowl. She pulled the small blanket from the back of Augie's chair, wrapped it around her shoulders, and headed for the path behind the house.

As she walked from the hill down to the chapel, she couldn't see the dog anywhere. She took a deep breath and closed her eyes for a moment, remembering Augie's casket. Following the path to the chapel, she kept calling for the dog. She stepped through the ancient arched doorway into the empty stone church.

"Ombra?" she called, her voice sounding hollow against the bare stone walls.

Flickering light through tree branches beckoned her out the back. She felt hypnotized. Long gravestone shadows darkened the path of the small cemetery on the right. She walked past the weathered stones until she came to the freshly turned sod.

There was Ombra, slumped over the highest spot of dirt. His face rested on his paws while his back legs sprawled out behind him, his toes reaching into a pile of dead leaves. His big dark eyes darted toward Carolyn as she approached.

"I brought you water, Ombra."

When Carolyn had gotten to within three feet of him, Ombra began a low growl.

"It's OK, boy. I'll just put it over here."

As she set down the bowl and cutlets, she noticed the headstone next to Augie's grave.

HERE LIES
~ ELEGANZA ALIBERTI~
BELOVED MOTHER~ DEVOTED WIFE

Tears welled up in Carolyn's eyes and her throat ached.
"Eleganza was his wife's name, too?" She choked.

As the last light of day disappeared into what Carolyn knew now to be the deepest, darkest dungeon of hell where serpents breathed out noxious fumes of sulfuric gas and suffered torture in deep rivers of molten lava, Ombra lifted his head and wailed.

Carolyn collapsed to her knees holding onto the cold, weatherworn headstone of Eleganza's grave and cried, "Why didn't he tell me? I would have never changed her name!"

When Ombra's wail crescendoed into a howl, Carolyn wailed with him. She could finally cry for Augie. Since his death, she'd been frozen. A cold, gray rock.

Her hot tears flowed in a torrent now, through the barely cooled traces of the many thousands that had come before. Their macabre euphonic opera reverberated through the hills and valleys for hours until Carolyn exhausted herself. She sat numb and silent a long time, listening as Ombra kept on with his devoted vigil.

After pulling the water bowl closer, and not met with any growling, she shook out the blanket and laid it on top of the dog. She rubbed Ombra's head and neck, apologizing for the loss of his master, her apologies sounding empty and worthless, even to her. With still no growling, she laid her head on Ombra's back and continued to pet him.

Perhaps Ombra was comforted or perhaps he sensed Carolyn's grief, too. It was impossible to tell. She situated the blanket over them both and fell asleep right there in the dirt, feeling guilty for finding more comfort in the warm, pitiful howling animal than she'd known in a long, long time. Their sorrow and grief shared the same bitter melody that dark, dismal night.

Chapter 23

As Carolyn left the inconsolable dog that morning, she turned back, calling to him one last time. There was no response. The buzz of a scooter caused her to hurry to the house in time to see Ramone from the marina scooting up the long drive. Dirty and exhausted from spending the night on Augie's grave, she rested at the stone bench and waited.

"Augie's solicitor wants to see you tomorrow. Noon. Can you make it?" asked Ramone.

"Why?" asked Carolyn over the sound of the motorbike's engine.

"About things I do not know," said Ramone.

"OK. I still have the Vespa here. Can you please tell Fausto I will return it tomorrow? I haven't had a chance."

"Carolyn, no worry. Fausto knows you have it. No worry." His voice died off as he gave his bike full throttle and drove away with a wave goodbye over his shoulder.

Carolyn knew she couldn't leave the vineyard until she could figure out what to do with Ombra. She hoped the lawyer would help with that, she thought as she watched Ramone drive away with a trail of dust behind him. As long as she was going to town, she made a mental note to stop at the yacht and pick up a few things.

Later that afternoon, she headed back to the chapel with more food and water. As she walked up to Ombra, she noticed he hadn't moved from his place on the grave. Neither the food nor the water had been touched.

Ombra looked over and then closed his eyes. Carolyn knelt

THE KISS GOODNIGHT

down to pet him. This time the dog didn't growl. His eyes didn't dart, and he didn't flinch. He just lay there with his eyes closed.

"Ombra, you have to drink," she said as she dripped water on the dog's mouth with her finger. After the third drip, he opened his eyes, wiped his tongue on his lips, and then closed his eyes again. After that, he ignored her. Carolyn moved the bowl close to his face and got up to leave.

"Ombra, Augie would want to you eat and drink, you know. Please," she said.

Halfway back to the house Carolyn heard an unfamiliar sound. A faint thundering from the ground caused her to stand still and listen. The sound resembled a sound between rumbling horse hooves and a harrumphing snore.

She looked through the rows of lush grapes on either side of the path until she spotted the rustling vines of something tearing its way toward her. The grunting grew louder as its source broke into her row.

Running straight toward her was the 250-pound bristle-haired body of a wild boar. His large heavy head and sharp curved tusks looked disproportionate on his short stubby legs. His pounding hooves and panting snorts and squeals maneuvered toward her with blurring speed. She stood frozen, her eyes growing wider with each approaching lunge of her likely death.

Just as it crossed into her path, a black blur flew in front of her. Ombra plunged his bared fangs into the beast's snout and dug his hind legs in the dirt. An ungodly shriek pierced Carolyn's ears as the wild boar swung its head back and forth, thrashing the dog from side to side. The giant pig shook Ombra loose, flinging him five feet in the air as if he were nothing more than a sparrow.

Ombra yowled as he thumped to the ground and knocked into the vine post. Without a second's hesitation, he snarled, scrambled to his feet, and charged back into the fight.

As the boar's long, hideous tusk pierced Ombra's flesh, Carolyn heard a soft thumping rip. The dog let out a high-pitched yelp as he viciously bared his teeth. Crazed, he snapped into the air, slashing his teeth together as fast as a bug zapper on the fourth of July, until he landed a bite.

With Ombra's teeth sunk into the boar's snout, he dug his

back feet in the dirt and hunched down. He yanked the boar's nose back and forth with fierce tears.

A lightning bolt of raw adrenaline rushed through Carolyn. In the eerie chaos of hog squeals, grunts, dog yelps and growls, she pulled the blade of her snake dagger from its sheath, held it high in the air then drove it into the boar's side.

"You bastard!" she yelled.

An ear-piercing squeal echoed through the vineyard.

Carolyn pulled out the thin blade, closed her eyes and lifted the blade and using both hands, plunged it in again until she could feel the scratching bristle of the hog's back under her hands.

The boar staggered forward, hard, knocking Ombra off balance. The enraged beast stomped him several times with its front hooves and then wheeled around like a drunk that had stayed too long at the club.

Carolyn rushed to Ombra and knelt down next to him. She turned to watch the boar lope off, head down, grunting toward the safety of the distant woods.

She knew about the beasts that roamed the hillsides of Italy. She'd heard Augie talk about vineyards and grain fields being wiped out in a matter of hours by a sounder of wild boar.

Carolyn moved her hand over Ombra's leg and applied pressure over the ripped flesh where he'd been gouged. Though it wasn't bleeding much, the thick fluid oozed between her fingers. When she was sure the wound wasn't fatal, she patted his head and sat in the dirt with him for a few minutes to catch her breath.

She stood to her feet and tried to pull the dog up by the neck.

"Come on. Let's go home," she said to him.

Ombra gazed up at her with his sad, dark eyes and then closed them.

"Come on, boy. Please?"

Carolyn shook her head. As she turned to leave, the dog slowly got to his feet and limped over to her. They walked back to the house side by side.

Ombra finished off the platter of chicken and Carolyn had to fill his water bowl three times before he'd had enough to drink. After he'd finished eating, Carolyn carefully wiped his leg with warm water

THE KISS GOODNIGHT

and a towel. The dog barely flinched. While applying the antibiotic ointment, she decided to take him to the vet the next day.

When the last of the sun disappeared that evening, Ombra lifted his head and moaned. Carolyn patted him, being extra careful of his leg. In a soft, soothing tone, she began to talk to him about the vineyard. She told him stories about how much Augie had loved him, and about other brave dogs, too.

He lay his head on her foot and sighed.

That night, he followed her up to the guest room and lay down in front of the door. Carolyn listened to him sigh deeply, off and on, until she fell asleep.

Chapter 24

Before dawn the next morning, Carolyn found herself wide awake. On her way downstairs, she looked around for Ombra. He was nowhere. As she entered the kitchen, she stopped, frozen in fear. The door stood wide open, and she heard padding footsteps scraping outside on the veranda. She gripped the countertop for support and trembled in alarm.

Ombra walked in. He looked at her, turned around, and then pushed the door closed with his nose.

"Well, now, there's a new trick," she said with a sigh of relief. "You gave me quite a start!"

Her first instinct was fear that someone had broken into the house. Someone like Andrew. But that was crazy. She knew Andrew was dead.

"I guess it'll take a while before all that's unearthed from my subconscious... if ever," she sighed.

A small clump of crusted dirt fell from Ombra's paw and a thin layer of dust covered his legs and belly.

"You've been up to see Augie, again?" She asked, as she held her coffee cup high to balance it.

"I'm going to splash you, if you don't move."

Ombra stepped aside and then followed her to the veranda.

Purple shadows from the misted valley bled away as the mango glow of dawn peeked soft and easy over the horizon, like a romantic old love song.

Ombra took his place next to Carolyn, ready for a treat or a scratch, as the cool air grew warmer and the vineyard began to come alive with morning sounds.

Carolyn sighed as she tore Ombra a corner of toast and slathered it with honey for him. Augie would be happy. He'd always wanted Ombra to like her.

After two cups of coffee, Carolyn showered and readied herself to head into town. Her shorts were clean and dry, but she'd thrown away her torn blouse. She pulled another shirt from Augie's closet, rolled up the sleeves and cinched a belt around her waist. The mirror reflected a puffy billow around her rear-end. She smiled to herself.

No snide comments from Andrew.

She grabbed the keys to Augie's old green pickup truck and headed out the door. Ombra limped behind her. She loaded the Vespa in the truck bed and before she could close the lift, Ombra jumped in with it.

"You can ride up front with me if you like, Ombra," she said to the dog as she scratched his head.

But Ombra lay down and gave a quick bark indicating he was ready to go.

As they passed the small Paganelli farm, she looked up and saw Mr. Paganelli sitting on the porch with a shotgun balanced across his knees. She honked twice and watched as he jerked his head from a nap. He took a quick look around and then waved.

"Good thing Andrew's dead," she told Ombra through the back window.

She smiled but remembered the week-long watches at sea, catching catnaps when exhaustion overtook her and felt sorry for Augie's loyal neighbor.

Fausto, the young man in charge of the Vespa stand, was sitting, bored, under the umbrella that shaded his small wooden kiosk when they drove up. He'd already let down the tailgate by the time she walked around to the back of the truck. Ombra made no motion to get up. As Carolyn reached in to help Fausto unload the Vespa, Fausto's arm brushed against her. Ombra pulled back his upper lip and growled.

"Ombra! You've known me for years, you old bear," Fausto said. "Looks like he has a new charge."

He nodded to Carolyn before looking back at Ombra with a slight uncertainty.

Fausto wouldn't take money for the Vespa rental.

"For Augie," he said with a bow of his head.

As Carolyn got back in the truck, Fausto reached in and gingerly scratched the dog's ears.

"You take care of your new lady, you grumpy old hound," he said before smacking the truck fender twice.

Next stop, the vet. It was with a lot of coaxing that Ombra hopped down from the truck bed and then was pulled in to see the vet. Carolyn had to leave the room when the vet poked and prodded Ombra's wound. Funny how the thought of a dagger slicing into Andrew's neck didn't bother her at all, in fact made her smile. But the whimper of a dog at the vet and she had to go outside.

"All done," the vet called out the front door of his office fifteen minutes later.

"Seven stitches. Give him these antibiotics twice a day. Hide them inside these liver treats and let's see him back here in seven days."

He handed her the small package.

"Ombra's lucky. A full-grown boar can gut a dog his size. Sounds like you'll be hosting a hunt party come September. Mmm, Pappardelle Cinghial, perfect on a fall day. It's Italy's national dish, you know. Wide ribbon pasta and tomato-boar ragu. Mmm," he said without pausing.

"Glad you'll be sticking around, Carolyn. I'll put this on Augie's account."

With that, Ombra nudged Carolyn's arm, in an "it's time to get out of here already" way.

"Thank you, doctor," she said, trying to hold onto Ombra.

Carolyn followed the dog back out to the truck, wondering what the vet meant about sticking around. Now that Augie was gone, why would she stick around?

At her next stop, the solicitor's office, she found out what the vet, and apparently everyone else in town already knew.

"Good morning, Miss Carolyn," the lawyer said.

"Well, it's high on to noon isn't it? Sorry, good afternoon. I'm Enzo Gianni. How are you this glorious afternoon?"

THE KISS GOODNIGHT

"I'm fine, Mr. Gianni. Ramone from the harbor told me you wanted to see me. I do have a few questions about Augie's vineyard. Tomas left in such a rush, I don't even know what to do with Ombra," she said.

"Ombra is yours, Miss Carolyn, along with Augie's entire estate. You may do with him whatever you wish. Congratulations. Augie wanted this very much," he said.

"What?" She asked. Stunned, she mentally noted it was hard to get a word in edgewise this morning.

"Yes, dear. Shortly after you purchased the yacht, he came in here and set this in order."

"What about Tomas, and his other son, the doctor?" Carolyn asked.

"Augie was very lonely after his wife's passing. He never forgave the boys for leaving, and Augie could hold a mean grudge. Don't get me wrong. He was the kindest man I've ever known, but don't push him wrong. It's yours, Carolyn. All yours. I'll have the final papers drawn up by Wednesday or Thursday of next week. Why don't you come by again on Friday and we'll have this all wrapped up."

"I just don't even know what to say," she said.

After leaving the lawyer's office, still in shock, she drove the old pickup to the marina. Ombra jumped down from the tailgate and followed her, limping, to the dinghy. It was then that she realized Ombra's left leg was gashed in the same place as her own. She reached down and scratched his head.

"I know how you feel, boy," she said.

"Exactly how you feel."

Ombra sat in front of the dinghy with his nose held high, sniffing in all the ocean air. He loved sailing as much as Augie had.

Carolyn decided they would sleep aboard that night. She had many things to think about now. Not only the microchip, but also Andrew's death, and Augie's. And inheriting the vineyard? How will Augie's sons feel about that? She couldn't wrap her mind around it all. Griff even popped into her mind after Tomas's comment. She missed him. Yes, she would stay aboard The Kiss Goodnight and think.

But as the sun dipped lower in the sky, Ombra decided he

wanted to go visit Augie's grave. He stood at the railing and whined until Carolyn lowered the dinghy. He jumped in and waited while she shook her head and packed a bag.

As she drove up the dark road, she spotted a light on Old Man Paganelli's front porch. She gave the horn a light tap and saw a figure raise a shotgun in hello.

He certainly took his job seriously.

Carolyn felt guilty knowing she was in no danger due to Andrew.

"He's fish food." She tried to cackle and then laughed at her effort.

"I'll have to figure out a way to let Mr. Paganelli know I'm safe."

As soon as she stopped the truck in the side yard, Ombra jumped down and took off. He dipped and bobbed on three legs as he headed toward the chapel.

"Ombra!" she called, to no avail.

"I am NOT going out there to fight wild pigs tonight!"

But she was already wondering where she should look for a flashlight. The night was quiet with only a slice of crescent moon hanging overhead. Not nearly enough light for another boar battle.

A distant faint blue streak flashed in the heavens before a trail of glitter glowing from behind, faded out into the night sky.

"A falling star," she said.

"Augie," she let his name linger, before it faded into the night sky, as well.

"Thank you, Augie. For everything."

She knew she couldn't take the vineyard. It belonged to his sons. But she would look after it, and Ombra, until it was all sorted out. As she reached the back door of the house, she heard Ombra howl from the chapel, just once. As she listened for the next howl, she finished pouring a glass of wine. She'd just begun looking through the cupboards for a flashlight when the door opened and Ombra walked in.

"Good boy!" she said while giving his neck a rough rubbing.

"Good boy."

***

Carolyn met with the solicitor the following Friday. And before she could even begin with her concerns, he began talking non-stop again.

"The boys have been notified of the contents of the will, Carolyn. They've signed off. They have no interest in the vineyard. Never have. I understand they are both quite successful in their own right. Augie could never grasp the fact that they might be happy outside of the vineyard or outside of this small town. He was a stubborn man. The kindest man I've ever known, but stubborn. It's all yours, Carolyn. I hope you enjoy it. The dog, too. Sign right here."

Carolyn signed the papers.

After a few weeks of settling in, Carolyn and Ombra worked out a routine that was temporary in Carolyn's mind. She knew she'd be seeing Tomas again. Andrew's trail would grow cold, and he'd be back to get any information, as insignificant as it might be. Little did he know, she had a great deal of significant information. At any rate, they would discuss the vineyard then. And perhaps the microchip. She wasn't sure.

One morning she followed Ombra to the chapel and dug a small hole at the foot of Augie's grave. The snake dagger bracelet lay next to her on a small leather bag she'd found in the garden shed. As she dug, Ombra circled the bracelet, growling and baring his teeth. She couldn't help but wonder if he knew that it was Andrew's blood, mixed with the wild boar's that was smeared on the handle.

She held her gold anklet to her lips and closed her eyes. Tears rolled down her face as she kissed the chain and threw it in the bag. She had no idea what information might be on the chip, but it didn't matter. Mike was dead. Andrew was dead. Augie was dead. She'd leave it buried where it couldn't cause any more trouble.

A moment later, not bearing the thought of burying her chain, she pulled it back out of the pouch, snapped open the clasp and pulled out the tiny microchip. She tossed it in the bag with the dagger. After she covered it in soil, Ombra pawed more soil over it and lay on top of it. Carolyn laughed.

Summer drifted into fall and Ramone arranged a Cinghiale hunting party. The beasts had destroyed three entire acres of the vineyard already and hadn't had their fill. Though the vineyard didn't feel like hers, she felt responsible until she heard from Tomas or his brother. So far, she'd had no response from any of her inquiries.

She found herself looking forward to the hunting get-together. It had been quiet and lonely up here with only Ombra to keep her company. She was beginning to understand why Augie so desperately wanted his sons here. The shriveled fruit and dry withered vines that remained after the wild boar carnage only served to further remind her of her crumbled, lost romance with Griff.

So, when Ombra stood in the kitchen and barked twice, alerting her that someone was coming up the road, Carolyn grew excited to greet her guests. They walked out to the stone bench, and with Ombra taking his position under Carolyn's arm, they waited for them to arrive. Only a single Vespa engine sounded through the valley and when it came into sight, Ombra barked twice again. Carolyn reached over and scratched his head.

"Good boy," she said. "Did you know you are my favorite boy?"

Carolyn cupped her hands over her eyes and furrowed her brow. There was only one lone rider, not the hunting party she'd expected.

"Maybe an early bird?" she asked the dog.

As she squinted in the sun, the hunched-over form of the rider came closer into view. She stood frozen to the spot, not daring to breathe, as each beat of her heart drummed increasingly louder until the deafening throb pulsed through her ears.

She opened her eyes wide in an effort to see through the slick of gathering moisture. A chill raced over her skin in the heat of the morning sun and the hair on her neck stood straight up. And when she *was* sure, a choking sob whimpered through the vineyard's silent acres of dormant vines and lifeless leaves as she ran toward him.

It was Griff.

Chapter 25

A few weeks later, an old woman, wearing purple paisley harem pants and a matching flowery babushka, took a little longer than her fellow worshippers did to get up from her prayer rug. Her knees were swollen stiff with phlebitis. As she passed from the coolness of the mosque into the afternoon sun, she shook her head at the idea she might be getting old.

"Hayir," she said.

A sudden strong urge compelled her to treat herself to lunch. She had the "touch," so she never questioned these compulsions, especially when they involved anything as innocent and enjoyable as a street lunch.

As she took a bite of the nice grilled fish sandwich with extra mayonnaise, she glanced down at the old page of the Hurriyet Daily News wrapped around her flatbread. A small dollop of mayonnaise clung to her lip.

Noting the date, she tilted her head to the side and thought back to that day. After reading a disturbing fortune that morning, she'd spent the rest of the day praying at the mosque. She shook her head from side to side and the mayonnaise plopped to her purple shirt.

As she took another bite of her sandwich, a short article at the bottom of the newspaper page caught her eye.

While reading it, the memory of the lovely American lady flashed in her mind and she gasped, inhaling the bite of fish. She began coughing and choking and before anyone realized she was in trouble, she passed out.

As the woman fell backward from her chair, the paper caught in an upsweep of wind and blew out over the Port of Istanbul.

The headline read:

Unidentified man pulled from the Bosphorus Strait

At the mouth of the Marmara Sea, the staff of the Barcu Zutar, a pleasure craft on a day cruise, rescued a drowning tourist. Although he appeared to be injured, the man refused medical help at the scene. He was last seen getting into a taxi near the Sarayburnu Iskelesi ferry dock. No police report was filed.

The End

A Note from Carol Goodnight

Thank you for reading The Kiss Goodnight. If you enjoyed it, please take a moment to leave a review at your favorite retailer such as Amazon USA. Please check out these other titles by Carol Goodnight.

amazon.com/author/carolgoodnight

BOOK 1 in the Carolyn Wingate Novella Series

A KISS IN DARKNESS

Broken-hearted from her CIA brother's accidental death, Carolyn Wingate, a successful Midwest construction executive, returns from his funeral to find that before his death he'd mailed her a lovely gold-and-diamond chain. Overcome with grief, she runs from everything she's known in a desperate search for solace.

Under the gentle swaying moss in the beguiling city of New Orleans she meets and falls in love with Andrew, a handsome, wealthy blue blood.

But a boat crash in the murky depths of a secluded bayou begins a string of perilous situations where Carolyn finds herself running again.

BOOK 2 in the Carolyn Wingate Novella Series

THE KISS GOODNIGHT

On the run from her crazy ex, Carolyn Wingate finds the gentle waves and sunny shores of the Ligurian Coast of Italy a safe place to begin life again. A new yacht, new friends, and a funny new love almost let her forget the unhinged billionaire that can't seem to let go.

Almost...

BOOK 3 in the Carolyn Wingate Novella Series

KISS OF THE NAKED LADY

Two sublime seasons have passed and life for Carolyn Wingate couldn't be better. Griff follows her to the vineyard with a marriage proposal and a promise to love and care for her forever.

But the quick report of rifle fire and several bullet wounds set Carolyn on a new path...

A path of revenge.

A short story inspired by a character in A KISS IN DARKNESS

LADY CE'CIL

As Lady Ce'cil strokes the deep scar gashed through her forehead, over her eye, and across her cheek, she slips through time to the stagnate bayous and bald cypress hammocks of South Louisiana. It is in the sweltering summer of 1922 where she achieves fame in the hyperkinetic world of jazz in New Orleans at the sacrifice of love.

Like my Facebook page ~ Author Carol Goodnight

Made in United States
North Haven, CT
29 May 2024